Sleepwalk Society

A Novel

Kendare Blake

Martinez, Georgia

This book is a work of fiction. Names, characters, places, and incidents are a product of the author's imagination or are used fictitiously. Any resemblance to actual events, locales, or persons, living or dead, is coincidental.

P.R.A. Publishing
P.O. Box 211701
Augusta, Georgia 30917

ISBN 13: 978-0-9821407-1-0

Printed in the United States

Acknowledgments

ALTHOUGH IT WOULDN'T BE INACCURATE TO THANK EVERYONE I'VE EVER met and everyone I haven't met yet, it would take up too much space. Therefore, I'll limit the list to those who have had a direct impact on this novel. I am deeply indebted to the following people for their guidance, inspiration, advice, and encouragement.

To Melissa Goldsmith and Susan Murray, always my first and kindest readers. To my brother, Ryan VanderVenter, who never lets me quit. To my tutors and peers at Middlesex University: Sue Gee and Linda Leatherbarrow for their expertise and Martina Olander, Gail Tiwari, Barbara Erskine, Yoshiko Obayashi, and Robert Clough for their careful eyes and insights. To Chase Buzzell, J. Eric Johnson, and Nick Jones, who also read. To my agent, Joan West. To my parents, for bankrolling me for more years than they counted on. And to Dylan Zoerb, for luck.

Chapter 1

OKAY, THE WORLD HATES US. THEY HAVE FLOWN PLANES INTO BUILDINGS and bombs are going off everywhere. Aside from the general displacement of the American psyche, the spring of 2002 is like any other spring in the northeastern United States. It is raining. It has been raining for a week—cold rain from gray clouds, beating with military precision right onto your head, intent on giving you pneumonia. Apparently, the memo to Mother Nature, April showers are to end in April, has gotten lost. What do I care?

I am pneumonia-free and only an observer to these drab surroundings; shut up in the top floor of this dormitory of flesh-colored bricks, with water sliding down the windows like mucus only to run across the ground, making the world slippery. Nine stories down, students who haven't finished up their final exams—all running against the wet onslaught behind the barricade of school-logo umbrellas—are skating along on the grass. It is stupid. The rain is coming down at an angle, so their legs are still being pelted—if they would just walk slower, they might save themselves some splashing. The beats against the window make my brain twitch; I can't take my eyes off of the students, milling around down there, made unidentifiable by the weather. There are so many of them, and more in universities just like this across the country. I try to pick out one or two with more confidence in their strides, more hurry in their steps as they go back and forth taking tests, but I can't. They all look the same, clothed in soaked sweatshirts and ambition. The law of numbers says they will not all make it, some will be pushed to the side, left to create the background for the ones who do. It is they whom I fear for and they who I fear to be; it has to be much better to be above them, to have the ability to say with pride, "I help people," or more discreetly, "I have money." Those pushed aside will crowd around these declarations, clap and grit their collective teeth because all their lives their parents and the media have promised them that they wouldn't have to be part of the crowd.

Some of them will always believe that promise; some of them will spend decades scraping for whatever it was that they placed above everything else: a possession, a job, or a love. I put my hand against the glass to shield them from my eyes and feel them struggling against my palm. For some of them, that struggle will come to be romantic—the climb more important than the summit. Maybe they are the lucky ones—having goals and learning to like the fight for perfection. Behind me, the door opens and closes. It is Terran, my best friend of 7 years, who is now my college roommate, back from her own race across the sloppy campus. She cuts a great picture against the open doorway, with her golden hair, in her wet jacket. If I were a 13-year-old boy, I'm certain that I'd be having one of those slow motion Phoebe Cates-climbing-from-the-swimming-pool-type moments. Terran is the kind of girl that evokes envy in everyone but me, and I know that I will probably end up as the first member of her fan club.

"Violet?" She says it like she can't see me standing by the window—like I'm hiding. I don't move at the sound of my name, which my parents picked out before they saw me. Now it is like a joke. A plain girl having a name that is a color. One of my boyfriends in high school said that the only color on my face was in my eyes and that the color resembled a faded dollar bill. He added that they would look good if only they could express feeling. He was right about the color. I stood in the bathroom one day with a wad of crumpled one-dollar bills just to make sure. Funny how one-dollar bills are the ones that fade. The hardest working of the money system with the least value.

"Violet?" Terran calls out again. I am not really listening, instead of hearing the right pronunciation of my name I hear "violent?" and I answer anyway.

"Are you all packed?" she asks.

I glance around the room, the walls white except for leftover poster tack, the beds stripped bare with our bags and totes piled on top. The remnants from our first year at college.

"Yeah." I finally respond.

She gathers up her stack of belongings—much larger than mine, and flips off the lights. "Let's get out of here," she says.

Before I go, I take one last look down at the ground, one last look at the campus. Some of these college kids are really in their element. Those scruffy dreadlocked white girls with revolutionist sweat in their armpits must be so sad to see the term end. What will they do all summer in their sparrow-fart hometowns without their fellow activists to shout beside them? What will they do when they discover that their kind of passion doesn't outlast an undergrad degree, unless you join up with PETA?

Terran shouts to me to hurry up. I turn and follow her down the shadowy hall—running water making designs on the walls—and bump her shoulder like I've done since we were 12. She smiles at me. I've heard it said that friends scatter and that nothing lasts forever—that the people whose faces you look into now will be strangers in your address book someday. But she's been with me since junior high, and those words read like words from my econ textbook: dry, and with no real meaning beyond the cognitive.

◆◆◆

It is a long drive home from school, 5 hours in clear weather. Terran's Mercedes cruises along at 80; she's not mindful of the rain. She is daring the cops to have the nerve to pull her over in the downpour. She turns down the radio. Taps a cigarette out of her pack, lights it, then passes it to me. I don't smoke, but I don't think she wants me to outlive her. She crumples up the pack and rolls down the window to toss it. I catch her arm and reprimand her with, "Save the Planet." She smirks—ha ha—funny little joke as we drive along an interstate decorated with plastic bottles and fast food wrappers. She drops the pack into my outstretched hand and we feel good about ourselves, doing our part to postpone the day when we all get caught in our own wasteful trap—maybe we'll be able to gnaw our legs off and get free, and maybe we won't. The point is, this crumpled cigarette pack will find its way into a proper landfill with a lot of trash instead of in a ditch with only a little.

"You're pale today," Terran says, "even more than usual."

I glance at myself in the side mirror. The gray of the day has passed itself onto me like I'm a chameleon—my brown hair looks silver instead. Terran asks how I did on my finals and I shrug. It doesn't really matter how I did. I didn't declare a major this year, just filled my time with exploratory nonsense. I even took bowling and am now the proud owner of a 135 bowling average. I don't have to ask her how she did on her tests because she always does well; besides, I know what she really wants to talk about. On our way out of the parking lot we passed a boy scampering up the sidewalk with the other idiots, his lower half soaked from carrying a laughably small umbrella and a dozen roses. Terran stopped because she knew that boy was my former boyfriend, Brian. I told her to keep going.

Two weeks ago I found him making out with Katie Quinn—a girl from our floor—on the living room sofa when I went to his house looking for a lost notebook. Terran wanted details the moment I told her, which are, I suppose, what a best friend would want. Receiving no details, she settled instead upon a barrage of canned questions:

"How are you feeling?"

"Fine," I replied.

"Are you angry?"

"No."

"Do you want me to kick him in the balls?"

Although that would be funny, again, "No," I said.

Now she's asking them again, only this time being very careful, because after the flowers and my own avoidance, she thinks that just maybe he broke my heart, when really I just didn't want the wet roses or a damp armrest from the rolled-down window. So, I try to pack the belated details into my answers, but they're no longer enough. She wants more, always more. I do not have the energy to make things up—not today anyway.

If I were to tell her the truth, I would have to say that when I saw my boyfriend of 4 months messing around with a girl from my dorm, a scant 12 inches from my misplaced notebook, the first thought that entered my mind was: Hey, there's my notebook! There was no screaming, no tears, no feelings of inadequacy, which are surely the way that a normal girl would respond if she were betrayed by a boy whom everybody wants. It is not normal that these feelings won't come. I could freak out and quit school, cry a lot and maybe get back on Prozac. It would be one outburst that everyone would understand, an injury that would put me on the sidelines and out of a game where there are no winners. Of course I don't tell Terran this. She definitely would not get it, not her, with her beauty and her life spanned out on a red velvet carpet. She wouldn't get it, so I don't say it, because I've learned fast enough that when you go around saying things that people don't get, they begin to think you're weird. And weird is bad, though I don't know why, if being unique is good. What's the difference between weird and unique? Nothing more than the degree of social acceptance.

"Violet?"

"What?" I say stupidly, while scanning my brain for a quick comment to appease her. I tell her that I wish Katie Quinn would stop avoiding me. We were friends before Brian and it seems stupid for that to end over something that I care very little about. Terran squints in disgust, the wicked effect making her no less pretty.

"Who cares? There's nothing lower than a girl who will stab another girl in the back over a boy."

"It's not like we were best friends or anything."

"That's not the point. I don't care if you even know the other girl. I don't care if the guy tells you that his girlfriend is a frigid bitch who doesn't appreciate his genius. I don't care if you think he's the love of your life. If he has a girlfriend, he's off limits. End of story. When will girls get that? I mean, what do they think they're winning? All they're getting is a cheater."

I should really tell her to get off of the soapbox. In high school, she was a renowned boyfriend-stealer. But she speaks with the vehement conviction of the reformed, so I just smirk and say: "Yeah, that would be great. Then we could all stop hating each other for having huge boobs."

That makes her laugh beautifully. Being a girl, I have the privilege of saying that she's gorgeous without questioning my sexuality. Boys don't have that luxury, and I pity them for the limitation. The comment about tits doesn't work to change the subject, however, and I wish something sudden would happen—like a deer in the road. But nothing is up to sacrificing its life for me today, so I'm forced to tell her that I already saw Brian, that we already talked, and that the drenched roses of today were actually a second offering. Or maybe they were for Katie, come to think of it.

Her questions are back and multiplying quickly, too fast for me to answer, and she's drawing her own conclusions in that annoying way that smart people have, so I have to cut her off. "Look, he showed up while you were at your Ethics final. He apologized; I declined. I gave him the flowers back and told him to have a good summer."

"You what?"

"Yeah, he's interning at Arthur Andersen, for all that's worth." The look on her face is not happiness, and the look on mine is probably an exact reflection. "What do you want me to say? That I screamed at him, then ate the roses and beat him about with the rendered stems?"

"Yes! Anything but let him walk all over you."

"How can it be walking all over me when I don't care?"

"You really don't get it."

"I really don't." I say defiantly. But neither does she. And it's beyond my energy to explain why I don't think that four-letter word that everyone's so obsessed over and that gets everyone into so much trouble and pretty much makes everyone behave like an ass can live in a place like this. Somewhere during dry cleaning, details, and missed meals, it flakes away and what you're left with is married people with a tolerable affinity for each other. That little four-letter word can exist only in poetry, or movies of 2 to 3 hours in length. Maybe in a mini-series.

This place of dull details and irksome obligations is a home only to other four-letter words, which are used much more frequently.

She turns the radio back up.

Chapter 2

THE RAIN FOLLOWS US—MOVING IN A STEADY SHEET FROM WHERE WE were to where we are. Terran suggests that we leave my stuff in the back so it doesn't get soaked and unpack it tomorrow.

It's a good plan because I'm drenched the moment I step out—a cold, stinging wet that weighs down my navy-blue hooded sweatshirt and makes me slouch. I wave over my shoulder as Terran's headlights retreat, heading to her mother's house on the hill, the white three-story spectacle that's visible for miles, a monument to her excellence in career and divorce.

I stand for a minute and look at my own parents' house. It stares back at me in two stories of red brick and green shutter, Doric pillars and tulip mixes. Despite the headlights, there is no one peeking out the windows or coming to the door. Maybe they knew I wouldn't need any help unloading.

When I get inside, I have a minute or two to watch the rain dribble off of my pant seam to form a symmetrical puddle between my shoes before my mother bursts out of the sitting room like an overzealous guest at a surprise party, her arms wide, ready to hug me with one arm as she holds a half-empty tumbler in her other. The hug stops 3 feet away, the smile falling off of her face so hard that I swear I can hear it bounce off the floor. "Hi, Mom," I say. She takes a drink as she looks at me, eyes wide with horror, like it isn't water that's leaking off of me but the last bit of my color, and I'm a translucent alien standing in her foyer.

"Violet, how many times have I told you to carry an umbrella?" she scolds.

I try to remember how many times as she turns away in a flash of peach satin nightdress and robe, returning a few seconds later with towels from the kitchen, the first of which goes under my feet to stop the puddle from spreading. When she bends down, she stumbles. That is not a good sign. Although my mother spends sixty percent of her life intoxicated, she never stumbles. My return must have shaken her straight to the bottom of the decanter.

"Where's Dad?" I ask. I am basically dry now, but the afore-promised hug hasn't rematerialized. I am sure we're both relieved.

"At the office." She pulls her robe tightly around herself, like I'm emanating waves of cold. She doesn't ask about the absence of the rest of my things, like she expected me to show up with one overnight bag—the guest at a bed and breakfast rather than a three-month tenant. The silence stretches out here, despite the fact that we haven't spoken since winter break, and she squirms in it. Most people squirm in silence, like just the fact that there's nothing happening is in itself dangerous. Not me. Silence is my armchair from which to watch the world. I try not to break it, but I don't have to; the grandfather clock beside us strikes 10 in its heavy annoying song of time passing, and that's our cue. She backs up, effectively opening my route to the stairs.

"You must be tired, sweetheart."

"I am."

"Then go right up to bed. We'll have all summer to talk." She clears her throat after she says that last part. As I shuffle past her, I think that it actually is nice to be back. It's comforting that nothing has changed although that's a stupid thing to be comforted by. I turn around, with half a mind to tell her so, but all I see is her shadow.

"It's good to see you, Mom."

"It's good to see you too, dear," she sings back at me, the expected response, sung a little too loudly to cover the clinking of tumblers and ice cubes.

◆◆◆

I've barely begun to daydream when there's a knock at the door. I'm surprised, but the surprise fades into curiosity when I see that it's Joey, the male element in the trio that consists of Terran, Joey, and Violet, in that order.

He flips on the light. "Did I scare you?"

"No, just surprised me. I thought you were my mother." I sit up and he comes the rest of the way in, pacing around. He's damp from the rain, his black hair shining, blue eyes flashing, and he looks like the storm itself. He looks around the room, his eyes flitting onto me and then off, like he's following the path of a fly. He rarely looks at me squarely. Despite the fact that I've known him almost as long as I've known Terran, I always get the feeling that the look of me makes him uncomfortable.

"What are you doing here?"

"I've been home for a week. I'm ready to kill my parents."

"I mean why aren't you over at Terran's. And don't act innocent and hurt. We both know she's your favorite." The innocent and hurt look slides off of his face, instantaneously replaced by an ogre-like expression that I know is an imitation of Terran's mother. I laugh. We both avoid Terran's house whenever possible. Her mother is a real bitch. Meredith. It's easier to sneer her name than just to say it. She's a woman with her chin constantly elevated. She's perfect. Smart. Tall. Rich. Well-bred. And she looks like she could be Terran's sister although that takes work. One more chemical peel and the next one is going to expose bone. I am convinced that she was never actually born. She must have sprung fully formed from someone's head, like the goddess of battle. Although her eyes are always watching herself in the mirror, or her daughter, or any attractive man in the room, she focuses primarily on two things: opportunities for herself and the imperfections of others. So, of course, she has never approved of Joey or me. Joey with his perpetual underachievement, and me, perpetually odd. And she's never bothered to hide her disapproval. She'll criticize my clothing or Joey's working-class parents as though she employs us. Never mind that I'm wearing Terran's cast-offs or that Joey's working-class parents own a tri-state shipping company that has run in the black for a decade.

"Did your mom know you were asleep?" Joey asks, snapping me into the present.

"I wasn't asleep. But I'm sure that she thought I was. Why?"

"Because she let me right in and practically shoved me up the stairs." He's grinning at me quite handsomely, but I know there are no implications in it. Terran is more than just his favorite; he's in love with her.

"She's drunk," I shrug. "I don't think Terran's coming over tonight."

"I came to see you anyway," he says, his eyes fall to the bed sheets. He stretches athletically, bitches about the past winter's lack of snow, talks with a limited vocabulary about frat parties at State U. His eyes are darting back and forth again, and I wonder what he must think as I sit watching him, not moving, not offering up anything. I can tell that it's bugging him. He wishes I would say something, so I ask him how his first year went. He tells me that he's still a psych major and on the baseball team but hasn't played much because he's been on academic probation since last term.

He's leaned back against the wall. He hasn't changed since I last saw him over winter break. His hair is still short and black, and he still dresses out of an ad for Ralph Lauren. The academic probation story tells me that he hasn't gotten any more ambitious. He's talking about things that don't interest me: cars, stories about vomit, upcoming parties—in a dull voice that tells me that they don't particularly interest him either. Joey has never had any particular talents or passions. I don't think he feels the need to cultivate any. As an only child, his inheritance of the family fortune is less speculation, more a foregone conclusion. He never worries about money—just about all the time that he has to spend it in.

He asks about my year, and I answer with enough simplicity to hold his attention, then tell him what he really wants to hear. "Terran's doing really well."

"That's great." He doesn't mean that. What he'd really like me to tell him is that Terran hates it, hates school, hates her Valkyrie mother and wants only him. I wouldn't tell him that in a million years.

"Is she seeing anyone?" The question is soft and hesitant. It comes from the mouth of a little boy, not from Joey himself. Joey himself is nothing more than urges without names wriggling beneath the skin.

"She is," I say to Joey. "But I don't know if she broke it off for the summer," I say to the little boy. He stands up. He looks out of my window at the rain, which sounds harder, if anything.

"I wish I never had to sleep." He's heavy with those words. What he means is that he wishes he never had to wait. Sleep is the enemy for someone like Joey, someone who wants to use up all of his time as quickly as possible.

"Joey?"

"Yeah?"

"What are you going to do with yourself after you're done romancing the beer bong?"

He doesn't look at me while he shrugs, then sits down on the bed with me and mutters, "Who says I'll ever be done." He looks down. "Yesterday I was out washing my car and my dad says, 'When I was your age, I knew that by the time I was 40, I wanted to have 2 houses, a sports car, and enough money to retire on. I had it when I was thirty seven.' What do you want, Joe?'"

"What did you say?"

"I didn't say anything. I knew he meant well and I didn't want to piss him off for once." He grins. "But I think it just pissed him off worse."

I smile at him and recline against my wall, painting the scene in my head. Joey's father, stout and frustrated, and Joey, his head hanging, mouth smirking, comfortable being a disappointment. But that question, "What do you want?" isn't so easy to answer. "What would you have said?" I ask him. He doesn't miss a beat.

"I would have said that I want to never turn 40." We give lazy, amused exhales. But then I realize that it is easier to imagine him dead than 40; my eyes can see his hair streaked with blood but never with gray. And if that much time does manage to pass, and I hear from someone that he died, of a heart attack maybe, or a car accident, the face that I'll see within that closed casket will be the one that's in front of me now. It strikes me that this is the only Joey that I ever want to know.

"What about you, Violet, what do you want when you're 40?" Instantly I see myself underwater, my hair gone dark like seaweed. It's surreal and I wish I were stoned, so this would make more sense. I wonder if this is a new truth, or if kids have always seen aging as dying.

"I want a house in the Hamptons and two kids. I want a devoted husband. I want to go to work in a suit."

"Whatever," he says. "You don't want any of that."

"It's a good answer, though." Forty. It's easier to imagine us dead than old—than to be the owners of some picket-fence baby boomer prize. But maybe that's only because Joey is reckless and

I'm already pale. "Hey wait, if your dad already has all of that money, then why's he still working?" Joey shrugs, and we chew on our lips for a while and think it over.

"I suppose I should let you sleep," he says finally, and I say, "yeah," but my legs are stretched out over his lap and he's been stroking my knees kind of nicely and he doesn't stop. He can't think of anything to do after he leaves here. I reach out to take his hand, not cold and dead at all but warm, and he comes closer, leans over me, and I feel like he's my father kissing me on the forehead at bedtime more than ten years ago; but he's not my father, and it's not my forehead that he's kissing. I was expecting one of his stupid kid-sister hugs, the kind where he squeezes me too tight and shakes me and messes up my hair. Instead there's a tongue in my mouth, and a body on mine, and he's never done this before. He's never wanted to do this before, and from the way his eyes are squeezed shut I know that he doesn't exactly want to be doing it now. But there was a mental coin-toss between sleep and sexuality, which for Joey is never a coin-toss at all. His hands slide under my shirt but I don't feel anything. In my head there's only a sudden rush of what-ifs and a mental checklist of birth controls. I have nothing to worry about. I can feel the frustration in his lips as he moves me around. He stops kissing me but leaves his mouth on mine, then arranges my arms in strange positions, where they stay frozen like a mannequin's. He pulls away, and we both laugh. He shakes his head and gets off of me, sitting on the edge of my bed with his face in his hands. When he finally looks at me, his expression is as close to a sheep's as is humanly possible. "I should go." I don't object, so he does. But before he walks out, he says to the floor. "Don't tell Terran."

"Don't tell Terran what." It's not a question.

Those blue eyes flash at me. He might call me the Sphinx if he knew what that was. He closes the door. I get comfortable on my back after he's gone. I know that I'll daydream for about an hour before I fall asleep. I always do, no matter how late it is. I spend sixty percent of my waking life daydreaming. I don't think that's normal.

Chapter 3

MORNING. IT HAS BEEN MORNING FOR HOURS AND STILL I LAY HERE, daydreaming off and on, sometimes listening for the world. What I hear is a soft clatter of pans downstairs as my mother makes breakfast. The slow Saturday steps of my father making his way to the kitchen. I can't linger any longer. My mother calling me down would be too annoying to bear.

So I break away from fantasies that feel more like memories and head into the shower to try to jump-start myself. It doesn't work. I'm still shuffling as I head down the stairs, eyeballing the lacquered piano, which has been comatose since I was 11. No one else plays. I think they keep it just to remind me that I'm a quitter—which isn't true—or at least not exactly. I was a competent pianist for as long as my mother drove me to lessons and watched me practice. But as her interest faded, so did mine; I suppose I never had any interest in it to begin with, rather I was feeding off of hers. And then I sucked her dry.

So I'm not exactly a quitter. For that you have to start. I'm more of a fader. Like one of those disturbing stuffed monkeys that clang cymbals together, my legs jerking to an eventual halt when someone forgets to wind me.

I can see my parents moving around in the kitchen. My father is sitting at the breakfast table, his nose stuffed into a newspaper. I'll check his face for newsprint when I kiss him good morning. My mother is opening and shutting cupboards, humming. She's in a good mood. It's nearly 9:30; I'm sure she's put on her mimosa-colored glasses by now and the world looks nice.

I don't go in yet. I want to tour the house, a quick inspection to see what has changed, but that would be too strange for them, and I'd have to hear about it all through breakfast—the strangeness. So I settle for a pause at my mother's mail desk, sliding my fingers along the walnut wood, fondly touching the silver letter opener. In the drawer is something I didn't expect: a box of latex gloves and a fluorescent light. She's made her own little anthrax detector. I have to smile at her ridiculousness. For the rest of the summer, I will fight the urge to sprinkle baking soda on my father's *Wall Street Journal.* "Good morning, Dad," I say, folding down his paper to kiss him on the cheek as I enter the room of last resort. I smile at my mother without showing my teeth, and she stops straightening the spice rack to grab my breakfast plate.

"Eggs Florentine" is what she calls the congealed yellow mass with green flecks that she sets down in front of me.

"Morning?" My father says from behind the headlines. "You've practically missed the morning. I thought you were going to sleep half the day."

The clock still says 9:30. My father doesn't know that morning ends at noon.

"Robert, leave her be," my mother says with no conviction as she pours me juice. I'm staring over the table at my father behind his paper, which he reads meticulously, despite the fact that the thing comes every single day save Sundays and the articles are suspiciously similar. The SEC has new guidelines for reporting operating income, one bold line promises. Like I care.

He's asking about my classes now, about my finals, about school in general. He throws these questions out in a string, to see if I can remember to answer them all, to turn a conversation into a report. I do my best to spit out the proper clicks and whistles, but he doesn't like that I'm still without a major and he hates my 3.2 average. He hates average period.

I kind of wince as he snaps his paper shut and folds it crisply into a small rectangle. Our eyes meet and I am struck. The breakfast table is gone. A canyon has risen up in its place. He's on the West end and I'm on the East. We shout words across to each other and the wind whips them away, carries them over, and translates them. When they reach me, the words are in Hebrew. On the other side, mine are probably in Swahili.

In the void between us is love. I can't shake the idea of a sparkly bridge. But there is no bridge. There is never any bridge. The love is there because it is like space itself; it must be there for the rocks to exist, even if it is only the by-product of American morality. To lose it would be to send one of us toppling into the dark, and both my father and I are unwilling to gamble about which one of us that would be.

Between my father and me, the question has never been love. The question is like and that becomes much more difficult.

When I was five, my father asked me if I wanted to see The Nutcracker over my holiday break. When my answer was a shrug of the shoulders, he patted my head affectionately, confused. When I was ten my father asked me what I wanted to be when I grew up. When I replied that I didn't know, he frowned. When I was seventeen, and had put off applying to any sort of school, he sighed, and when I ended up following my best friend to college without a declared major, he looked at me like I was a miscalculation.

You could say that I turned my father away from me through years of being odd. Through years of being the anti-version of the daughter he expected. Of course, the blame of me was lavished on my mother, being the only other person in the house, and the one who had given birth to me, and that blame is my mother's version of the canyon.

The moment is over, and the paper is back open. He's studying the movements of the Japanese yen against the U.S. dollar. "You should become a doctor," he mentions between pages. "It'll make you a good person."

For the rest of breakfast I'm wondering why it is that I'm not already a good person. If Einstein is right, and everything is relative, then I think that I am a relatively good person. I haven't committed insider trading this week, after all. But does the mere fact that you haven't lied, cheated, stolen, killed, beaten animals and small children, or given your neighbor the finger over the hedges make you a good person? That can all happen by chance. Or is it the will, the conscious choice to try, to strive to rise away from the human nature of the middle finger? I don't know that humans should be putting themselves at such odds with nature. It breeds trouble.

Two hours later, when Terran comes over to help me unpack, I'm still thinking about it. She looks fresh and life-like as she bounds up the stairs ahead of me with two of my four boxes in her arms. I move much slower—left panting and admiring behind her; she's run 2 to 6 miles a day since she was eleven. I've never seen the point of it. She'd probably be thin as a rail anyway, but now I know that she's been training all this time for heavy boxes and winding stairs. We throw the boxes into a corner. Everything except the clothes will probably stay packed until the fall.

Terran spins to the window and nudges it open, then throws me a T-shirt to stuff under the door. Before I can turn around she's got the white cocoon of a lit joint between her fingers. The

T-shirt is to keep the smell out of my mother's house. The window is a formality. The smoke would have long since sunk into the carpet before either one of my parents would venture into my room. The inhale burns, and I hate the taste, the sour dryness it leaves behind, but I smoke it anyway, because she gives it, and because it makes the daydreams harder to hold.

Terran's sitting on my bed beside me, hugging a pillow, her lids looking heavy. "What do you want to do?" she asks and I shrug, which makes her roll her eyes. She thinks that I shrug too much. She's told me so about a thousand times.

"How was your homecoming?"

The laugh that she laughs has no music. She's stopped passing the joint between us; it's pinched between her thumb and forefinger. She tells me the story of last night, how she came home to a house of ten to twelve people whom she never had time to count exactly. It was a dinner that had been eaten without her to celebrate her return. Meredith had played the perfect hostess—Clarissa Dalloway with blood under her fingernails. I tell her my story, with a few choice details omitted. I think she glosses over most of it. Only one word breaks through the weight of the drug. "You saw Joey? How is he?"

"He's fine." I'm thinking of his empty hands on me, empty lips. Restrained teeth.

"Same old Joey." I'm lying now, lying to her, my best friend. Does that make me less good? The fact that I'm lying for the sake of another friend, does that redeem me? These thoughts swirl around my stoned head. All logic is linear. All philosophy is circular. Five minutes later we're in her car, driving to find Joey. Before we left, Terran threw the joint out of the open window. I smiled as I thought of it striking one of my parents on the head and leaving them puzzled. As we walked out the front door we passed them sitting in the den. They stopped talking so abruptly that I know they were talking about me, and it occurred to me as I closed the door that although neither they nor I know any of my aspirations, they must certainly have their own set for me, a colorful map to steer me onto. It must be like that with all parents, and I suppose that must be love. Or something like it.

Fifteen minutes later Joey's in the car, and I relegate myself to the backseat, sitting in the middle to complete the triangle. There's another joint going around, I don't know where it came from, but it's too much too fast and I'm only taking tiny little breaths of it. The radio is loud. We talk over it, Joey and me in small circles around Terran, she with her intellect in large circles around us. It's easy and familiar. We talk about the same things over and over again because the same things always matter.

When Joey looks at me—rarely—there's something vaguely apologetic about him. Not in his eyes. His eyes are as sharp as ever. The apology is in the lines of his mouth, where it might be born, if we were alone. But somehow I know that we'll never again be alone, not the way we were only hours ago, and I'll never get to tell him that last night's fumbling was insignificant. It makes me sad, suddenly, and it feels like a shame, that time that we had as shadows together, wasted on all that touching.

"Am I a bad person?"

From the way they stop mid-sentence and look at me I wonder how long I've been silent. I have no idea. Time slips with thought. Seconds are long in the brain.

"What?" They both ask. They wanted to know what brought it on, the question which was new—random to them but heard by me for hours.

"Of course you're a good person," Terran says. Joey agrees, maybe for her benefit. He still looks worried; the question has worried him further.

"Why would you think that you're not a good person?" I don't bother to tell her that that's not what I said. "Haven't you always been a good friend to us?"

I consider her response. So is that what it means then, a good person is a good friend. Joey asks me what I've done; I must have done something to make me ask that, and behind his eyes there's a dare, which I pass up.

I'm quiet, thinking, but I must look appeased because they're talking again.

"I'm getting a B-plus," Terran says, and I snap back into the conversation. It must be a joke. Terran doesn't get B-pluses. Terran gets A's, and over A's. She can get an A on a 30-minute skim. But it's no joke and instantaneously we're all thinking of her mother. Joey might be thinking that Meredith is going to kill her, but the reality is much worse. One B-plus, the only B-plus, will brand Terran incompetent. She will be bound up, packaged, restructured. She is an under-performing tracking stock being refolded, as my father would say.

"It'll be all right," Joey says, wearing a sympathy mask over his real expression, the expression he gives only to her, never to me, not even last night. Joey's sympathy is born of lust, and I am sick thinking suddenly that all emotions of consideration are born that way, not born of a person at all, but of our own wanting.

They keep talking, feeding off one another, building themselves up, and slowly their voices are the same. I'm still in the backseat, listening incredulously to all the insecurities that she shouldn't have. I see them take form in smoke and rush against Joey's chest.

My head feels like a snow globe. I hope it's the drug; I hope it was laced, but there is no imagining the separate world in the front seat of the car, and I'm simultaneously shocked and jealous. That she should feel this way. That she should tell him first.

"Drop me downtown," I say and they look back at me through the smoke, struggling to focus in on my face.

◆◆◆

Downtown still feels drowsy from winter. There's a man in a turban sweeping the sidewalk of a deli, and it's nice to see. I thought that sort of thing only happened in books—men sweeping sidewalks in the early afternoon. He raises his head and watches me as I pass, his skin a warm brown in the sun, his shirt starched and white. He has polite eyes; he pauses his sweeping to let me go by, a small smile. He might invite me into the deli, but he's apprehensive, he let's me make up my own mind to keep walking.

There's very little noise on the side streets, just the swish swish of his broom behind me and I think of those polite eyes, flickering to my face and back to the ground. Before September 11, he might have said something, a greeting maybe, but now I'm a little too daunting. Me, an American girl, walking by herself. I think of turning around, of going into the deli and ordering something. I want to tell him through actions that he's not a country, even though he is—we all are, all of us—little pieces of countries, of movements, dangerous in groups.

Or maybe he doesn't speak English and the words would be wasted. I'd have to point out what it was that I wanted from behind the glass.

My throat is parched and I'm so stoned that I might walk into traffic. Someone says hello into my ear and I jump; my ankle gives out and I stumble.

He says he's sorry for scaring me, if that's true then he shouldn't have yelped into my ear. I tell him it's okay. There's a book bag over his shoulder, and his hair is fallen over his brow. I wonder where he came from. Down the street my sweeping man is gone, replaced by a mother with two children, walking out of a shop.

"Do you know where I can get a cup of coffee?"

So he's a tourist. Fantastic. That casts me in the role of local, how does that go? Friendly, helpful, with some kind of charm. Right. I smile at him, and he smiles back, a smile that has no doubt put countless girls on their knees before him. I'm unmoved, but I'm also thinking of coffee, so I tell him about The Stray Cat Coffeehouse and point my finger up the street.

"Join me?" he asks and I nod, his legs putting mine into motion. On the walk he's quiet, which agrees with me fine. I lack the saliva for conversation, and I can't think of any cute anecdotes about the city.

Inside The Stray Cat, a little, fragrant beatnik place, filled with abstract art, we order two house blends and he pays, but women's lib demands that I at least leave the tip. He hands me a cup and we walk to a table. I'm greedy for the heat and don't even add cream. It makes my throat instantly better but I hate the taste. Good coffee, bad coffee, I can't tell the difference. To me it all tastes like crap. I only drink it for the smell.

Sitting down brings us to the introduction stage of our relationship, so we exchange names. His is Brandon. He's here visiting family. I won't retain this information. He's a guy off the street, a tenant in the city, reaching out to a local to make his stay feel more like a home. I won't see him again. It's only a series of inquiries over coffee, and when my cup is drained, I'll return to my walk, or maybe catch a cab home. He asks what I do.

"This fall I'll be a sophomore in college."

"What're you going for?"

"I'm pre-med. I'm going to be a doctor." The lie is surprisingly gratifying. I could tell him anything, this tourist, and none of it would have any consequence. I want to do something really strange. Say something really strange. Anything. I want to become an amusing story that he'll tell to his friends back home.

But my coffee is gone. I take one last look at him. He has unruly brown hair and dark eyes. He's wearing a black dress shirt rolled up to the elbows. He's really very pretty. I should introduce him to Terran. Joey would kill me. Instead, I get up. He offers me a ride that I refuse, already walking away. But I glance back, once.

Brandon. A snapshot of a human being, filed away with all the others I'll forget. How many people have forgotten me over the years? People I've bumped into, or chatted with in elevators. We are all filler in other people's lives.

Chapter 4

I don't return to my house until after dark. When I get there, Terran's SUV is in the driveway, and I find her in my room, waiting for me, a magnanimous smile on her face and two outfits spread out on my bed like invisible flat people.

I ignore the clothes and look first at her. She's wearing a red halter-top with an open back, a silver chain threaded through the belt loops of dark jeans. Her hair is up in a blonde sweep. She's splashed with sparkle and beads. There must be a party. We must be going. She gestures impatiently toward my choices and I lower my eyes.

The outfits on the bed would both look much better on her, and they aren't as nice as what she's wearing. They also aren't what I would choose. I would go in what I have on. But she's really left me with no choice, having gone to all this trouble to turn me into a life-sized paper doll. I look the ensembles over, and all I really see are complications; too many accessories and too much flash. Sandals and silver bangles. Belts designed by names I should know. Leather bracelets.

"Sorry there's nothing here that's gray," she quips, and I look harder at the flat people on the bed. Are these really my clothes? Finally, I pick up the pair of jeans that looks the most comfortable and from the roll of her eyes I know she thinks I made the wrong choice.

"Where are we going?" I ask her, to keep her from pointing it out.

She traipses around the room as I change, telling me about the party. I'm half listening, with mm hmm's in the right places, trying to fasten the ridiculous bracelets she is forcing me to wear.

"He won't change my grade."

There's a scared kind of sad in her voice, and I look up. She's talking about her accounting professor, the one who's giving her the horrible B-plus. I'm surprised. Not that he won't change it. That she asked him to. I let the bracelets drop and discreetly toe them under my bed. She's telling me in a heartsick voice that it was unfair of him to make the last exam worth 30 percent. I'm hearing the same speech that I heard her reciting to Joey hours before. Has she forgotten that I was there?

She's tapping her fingernail against her teeth, something she started doing instead of biting them when her mother developed a penchant for manicures. If I were any other kind of friend, I'd put my arms around her. But as much as I love her, I'm not the touchy-feely type, and besides, she has Joey to blow sunshine up her ass.

I ask her what she did. She tells me that she swore at him, and I grin. Terran has dropped the f-bomb on a professor. I think it's hilarious and fantastic. She doesn't think so. She looks like she might be sick. Or maybe like she's already been sick.

"We're going to have a good time tonight," she says, and as she does, something crashes into the window, some night-flying thing in a cloud of fur or feathers, and my spine constricts and doesn't quite let loose again.

◆◆◆

It's the first party of the year. Everyone we know plus others are here. Cars are wedged into the driveway; SUVs lie buried in the pruned shrubs. The kid throwing it is an acquaintance from high school, Trent Finn. His parents are in Tuscany, the South of France, Barbados, some exotic, relaxing place that's unfit for accompanying children. The noise is audible from down the block, and I know that once we're inside we'll have to strain to hear each other, but I don't dread it. The first party for me is usually the best, because I'm not entirely sick of them yet, and I know that the others will be smaller. In the beginning, it's easy to feed off the crowd energy, people with lots of nothing to say, mixing together in a torrent of unexpected events. But over time, we get tired of other people. Other people get you caught up in things; they make it difficult to be what we are, indifferent, the sleepwalk society, drifting around the center of our lives. I know that by the end of the summer, it will just be us three, sitting in a car somewhere, talking less and less but louder and louder, one last rail against the new semester coming down to beat us over the heads.

The inside of the house already smells like beer and too many colognes mingling. People are standing around with drinks in their hands, talking. It's early. By the end of the night, bodies will be spread out in odd places, and draped over the furniture in odd positions like images in a Salvador Dali painting.

Terran infiltrates the ranks of the nearest group of girls like an absentee leader. They all watched her come in, each group, watched her with sly glances, hoping that she'd come to them and prove they were important. Julia Mason, an elegant redhead with a generous mouth, welcomes Terran to the circle and smiles at me. Later on her insecurities will make her cut us down of course. She'll say that Terran is conceited and that I'm a freak or some other unoriginal thing like that.

Small talk ensues, the small talk of college, of people sent out to learn in the world and come back to see who has become smarter. The talk is too intelligent for their tongues. They theorize about Ground Zero and conjecture about political alliances. They regurgitate brilliant half-truths touted by professors, each girl trying to steer the conversation toward her particular area of expertise, nodding at a friend's philosophical quote and then following it up with something from economics that's barely related. Nobody's really listening to anyone else. They're all just plotting their next intellectual coup.

I hope they enjoy it. In ten years they'll mostly be society wives, and their conversations will be of office gossip, fundraisers, and Botox. They'll be looking at their friends and wondering whether their husbands are screwing them.

I've stopped watching the faces of the girls. I don't need to. Terran is paying rapt attention. I'm looking around, catching snippets of conversations as people walk by, seeing faraway expressions and making up my own words to the scene. We're in the foyer, and Trent's parents have a lovely winding staircase up to and along the second floor, with a white banister and oak panels. At the top of it there's a lost-looking girl, sliding along the rail, a cup in her hand that sloshes on people below. Her hair is disheveled, and her shirt is askew. She's leaning against the railing and trying to come down the stairs without falling, but before her foot can even land, three boys are on her, talking and smiling, and before she can realize what's happened, they're herding her back the way she came.

I glance at Terran. She had been watching too. Whether she'll think 'slut' or 'poor girl' depends on her mood, but I can tell by the pretty wrinkle in her forehead that she's concerned. I squeeze her hand. Tomorrow may be the most self-reproachful day of that girl's life. Or maybe she won't even remember it—just wake up in a strange bed with a wet soreness between her legs that pulses into a panic.

We disengage from the gaggle in search of Joey. When we find him, he calls us 'his girls' like he always does in front of people and puts an arm around each of us, splitting us up with his body. He leads us into the den, his arm slipping lower on my shoulder, leaning against Terran, whispering something in her ear. They always do this, but now I'm annoyed, maybe because of today in the car. I shrug out of the three-way embrace, and they don't notice.

"Joey." The voice is a shout from the couch, clear over the thump of the music. The face it belongs to is familiar, and my brain does a quick flipbook skim before realizing that it's Brandon, the kid from the coffee shop. We're in front of him now, he hasn't noticed me yet as Terran gives all boys tunnel vision. As it turns out, the family that he's in town visiting (my brain pulls up from random-access), is Joey. They're cousins.

"Sure," Joey says. "You remember me talking about Brandon. I used to go up to stay with him and my aunt and uncle sometimes in the summer. In D.C."

Sure I remember. I remember the story. The name of the cousin was an unnecessary detail that I didn't retain. Terran is asking him questions, all the polite inquiries that I didn't make this afternoon.

"No, I graduated last year," he's saying.

"With a degree in what?"

"Ancient Literature."

"I didn't even know there was such a thing. It's kind of pointless, isn't it?" She's smiling when she says this, and her beauty will counteract her rudeness.

"Extremely pointless. Can't do a thing with it." He's smiling when he answers, and his beauty will counteract his idleness. He's still wearing the same jeans and black dress shirt. Terran is flirting with him, maybe to be nice, maybe for real. He's very pretty, so probably for real. I wonder if Joey notices. I wonder how much he trusts his cousin.

Brandon's eyes finally shift to me, and there's a surprised little shake in his irises, that I'm sure only I saw. He asks my name again though this'll be the third time he's heard it. Neither of us mentions our previous meeting. I don't know why. Maybe we're saving it up for later, our little secret, something to reminisce about when we meet again in 5 or 10 years. Or maybe it just isn't important enough to bring up.

The four of us sit, making us the only sane people. Everyone else is standing in a room full of sofas. We've been talking for only minutes when a boy alights on the arm of my chair.

He's a dealer. I can tell because he's cagey but not terribly high. He's grinning at us like an instant best friend and pulls a bottle out of his pocket. There's nothing in his eyes that isn't watchful and thirsty. I wonder how it feels to be a flesh-covered medicine cabinet. To have your whole being defined by the self-destructiveness of others.

It's ecstasy that he's peddling, and Terran is a taker. I pass. I've been designated to drive the SUV home later. The kid looks at me with disdain, like he would have been ashamed to sell to me anyway.

I know that the ecstasy probably isn't a good idea for Terran, not with Joey beside her looking at her like she's edible, but maybe that isn't fair. He's loved her for years and nothing has ever come of it. And besides, the pill, which she flashes at me (there's a butterfly stamped into it), is already down her throat. She hasn't eaten. In half an hour, she'll be rolling, and I don't have the patience to bird-dog her. I know Joey will be all too eager for guard duty, which is all right. He hasn't taken anything. Just beer. Maybe some coke.

Brandon gets up and he and Joey do that guy-handshake thing, which makes them look like 7-year-olds on a playground, and strides from the room. On his way out, he stops to talk to a boy by the stairs, a muscle-head in a too-tight T-shirt, who I instantly recognize as one of the ones who pulled the drunk girl back into a bedroom. The kid is gesturing, his mouth open in a constant, stupid grin, and then they laugh and go up the stairs together.

Terran has turned, seeing my interest, and now she turns back to me, her face full of disgust. The feeling rises in me as well, fluttering into my chest like a dying bird, and we shake our heads at each other with our eyes full of hate. But we don't get up. We don't stop him. It's like seeing a dog trapped in the median of a busy highway. You care. You may care intensely. But you don't stop your car. The righteousness of the feeling counterbalances the evil of inaction and you drive on. You measure yourself by the weight of your good morals. The funny thing is that you don't even have to practice good morals. Merely having them is enough to absolve you of guilt.

Terran and Joey are talking on the couch, ignoring me. Apparently the space between their couch and the chair where I'm sitting is an impenetrable crevasse. She's getting high. I can tell by the obsessive way she's starting to stroke his knee.

I drain my cup and tap it at Joey, who lifts his own, which is only half-empty. He smiles at me, and why wouldn't he with Terran giggling into his ear. I get up, walk through the melee, pause at the keg for a refill, and then walk on.

People are drunk now. They don't notice me as I go past, not a smile, no offer of a drink. I can parasite off of their conversations for minutes at a time, standing in a circle uninvited and not talking. They're oblivious. "What's a loser?" Someone asks. "A 30-year-old with a bachelor's degree," someone answers, and they laugh. I suddenly can't stand to be here.

I walk this great house that's big enough for twenty people and is inhabited by four. I find a quiet room with lots of windows. It's filled with plants and it feels slightly warmer; Trent's mom probably uses it to study botany or some damn thing. I shut myself inside in the dark.

The glass of the windows is cool and there are no stars. It stills my brain. For a moment, I'm content until the door opens and someone comes in, and if it's people coming in to copulate I resolve to stay quiet and hidden and just let them be done with it. They're eighteen and really drunk; it can't take long. But it's Brandon. I can see his outline coming toward me. My eyes have adjusted, but his haven't; he runs up against a bookcase before reaching me, and then he just stands, drinking his beer, looking out at the black. It's infuriating. I want to know what he's doing here, why he followed me.

"You like the dark," he says. "I like it too. There's nothing to see."

It's an odd conversation starter, I think to say, "What the?" "I thought you were upstairs," I spit instead, making my meaning clear. I want to score a jibe for the poor, defiled girl whom I didn't save.

He's quiet for a minute, and then says, "I locked her in a bathroom, Violet."

"You what?"

He doesn't reiterate and I don't ask again; we both know that I heard him. He takes a drink and snorts laughter into his cup. "You think I raped her."

I'd say no, but it would be entirely unconvincing. "You feel misjudged," I say with my mouth curling down.

He shakes his head at me—Joey's cousin—whom I met by chance and will now have to put up with until the end of his visit. "We're all misjudged. I suppose it'd be illogical for you to assume that I didn't rape her, after what you saw. But it doesn't matter. Judgment is the human condition." He reaches up, flips the latch and pushes the windows open, a cool, black breeze ruffles the room for a few seconds before rushing back out the way it came.

"So you didn't?"

"Now that we're talking, and for real this time, Miss Med Student, do you think that I did?"

I don't. Although nothing in him has changed aside from the fact that he has opened his mouth. I want to say, 'I am a med student, you jackass,' but what comes out is, "What are you doing in here?"

"I followed you. What are you doing in here?"

I shrug a reply, which he may or may not be able to see. I came in here to think, to get away, to wait for all the pieces of my silly brain to fall into place, to form a line, a figure eight, five rows of four, anything that's clear. I'm trying to find my way out of exploratory and onto a path. I'm searching for the answer, any answer at all, be it the meaning of life, the Holy Grail, or the Loch Ness Monster. Because at 18 I'm already behind schedule. We don't have time like we used to have time. I can feel mine burning away like the wax of a candle. Plus, I'm growing weary of having my father look at me with raised brows and imply that I'm shiftless. Reckless. Meandering. And not a good person.

I tell him all this. He probably won't get it, and that's fine. His role in my life is still that of transient; it's just been extended for a six-episode arc. But if he wants to be a sounding board, I'll let him be one. He moves closer to me. I move away, and hear his amused exhale. I want to keep him from asking something stupid, like 'are you scared of me all alone in this dark room?' so I ask, "Have you ever had a moment of clarity?"

"A moment of clarity?"

"You know, you'll be thinking about something, a problem maybe, and then all of a sudden everything is clear. For 30 seconds the ash of the world blows off, everything is brighter, more alive. Everything makes sense. You know exactly where you're going, and why." As I am talking, my voice takes on this ridiculous wistful quality, like I was reciting a fairy tale. So I cross my arms and speak lower. "It's like a 'duh' moment, like the answer you were looking for was there the whole time."

"I can't remember. But, I don't know if that's the kind of thing that you do remember. It's just a moment."

I can't remember having one either, but I say, "It's a life-changing moment. You don't think you'd remember that?"

"I don't think that life-changing moments exist outside of the grandeur of people's imaginations. Life is sneakier than that, in my experience."

I'm quiet. I don't know what I wanted him to say. Not that, that's for sure.

"Is that what you're in here doing? Awaiting an epiphany?"

I shrug, and he says he can't see it very well when I shrug in the dark. "This was a pointless conversation," I mutter. "Ten minutes of my life I'll never see again."

He's laughing and shaking his head. I think he's laughing at me. He grabs my empty beer cup and takes my arm.

"It was interesting. Nothing interesting is ever a waste of time," he says, leading me out of the room and straight into a jostle of increasingly intoxicated people.

I roll my eyes and sigh, and try to ignore the implications of the stares of the people around us, who see a beautiful boy and a strange-looking girl, coming out of a darkened room.

We have to weave through the people. If they were drunk before, now they're wasted, though I don't know how. We couldn't have been gone more than twenty minutes. They're much more animated: leaping around, throwing sculptures like footballs; someone puked on an oil painting, the bile does nothing to enhance the chiaroscuro.

We find the keg and refill, then wander, not back to our dark room, but just around. He takes me upstairs to check on the too-drunk girl, who is, sure enough, still locked in her bathroom fortress.

"Why are you visiting Joey?" I ask.

He shrugs. "I missed him. I was bored with D.C."

"How long are you staying?"

He shrugs again. "I don't know. Until I don't miss him anymore. Until I'm bored of this place."

They're simple answers, but I get the impression that they aren't simple thoughts. Brandon graduated from college last year, so that makes him 22, maybe 23. He hasn't mentioned a profession. He's in town visiting because he was tired of his home and he doesn't know how long he's staying. A neon sign goes on in my head that says something like "Loser! Bum!" But it flickers and goes out. I'm tired of boxing him in, first as a rapist and now as worthless.

He's leading me around through the rooms, back downstairs, drinking, chatting, and I like it, I like him, and I can tell that he likes walking with me too, sober people watching less-than-sober people—not being noticed. I think he's used to being noticed.

He's looking for cigarettes, accosting some poor kid passed out on the floor, slapping his pockets for the sound of plastic and ignoring the hands that come up to weakly defend the prone body. There's victory in the cargo pocket; he flips the kid over and takes out the pack, taps one out and offers it to me. I shake my head so he lights it himself.

"You're easier to talk to than I thought you'd be."

I look up at him, surprised, and he grins.

"Come on, you and Joey have been friends for how long? Don't you think he's mentioned you?"

I'm trying not to let this declaration change how I see him. I liked my perception of him, at the coffee shop, and now, walking through Trent's house together. But I realize that we've been talking from different bases. He's had a better vantage point this whole time, through Joey's descriptions of me. It feels deceitful.

I blink very slowly to keep from narrowing my eyes as I ask whether he knew me at the coffee shop today. I mean, Violet isn't that common a name, and he had to have had an idea of what I looked like.

He smiles and starts to answer, oblivious to my new suspicions, but he doesn't get a chance to finish because there's a sudden commotion outside the door. We go to see what it is and bodies are piling through the hall like sand through the waist of an hourglass. There's shouting. I hear Joey's voice, and we shove our way into the current. Brandon elbows us to the front.

Already there's blood. Blood on Joey's hands, face, shirt, and none of it his. It belongs to the kid on the ground, with his arms put up to guard his face, his knees drawn up to guard his body, which does no good. Joey is still kicking, and he doesn't appear to be growing tired. Someone should yell, "What's going on!" Someone should jump in, but nobody does, they're too busy straining to hear the sound of bone breaking.

I glance at Brandon. The emotions of awe and horror flicker back and forth on his face like they're images from a projector, and the effect is so strange that I don't know whether to laugh or scream, so I do neither.

The jeers and taunts from the crowd have stopped and a green sort of quiet has crept in. They watch as the kid gets beaten. Like Terran and I watched as the girl got raped. It's only when Joey reaches out to pick up the stone sculpture that people intervene, driving him back and wrenching it from his hands, taking it and the bloodied kid out of the circle with them.

Then they scatter somberly, their eyes alternating from the floor to Joey, who stands still in the center. I can hear the muttering—inaudible—and I'm disgusted with them, coming first to gawk and then to disparage.

Joey turns toward me and for a moment his still-enraged eyes are fixed only on a body that he intends to tear apart, and I think that perhaps I'll get to find out whether my insides are as pale and strange as my outside, but then he shakes his head.

I look him over. He's smeared with red, and there's a dark patch on the right knee of his jeans.

"Good thing you wore black," I say, motioning to his shirt, and he grins and says, "yeah," and sort of wipes his hands on his stomach and looks anywhere but at Brandon or me. It's like he doesn't know what to do next, and I think that maybe I should hug him or something, but I just can't quite bring myself to do it.

Terran is nowhere to be seen, and I know without asking that she's the cause of this. But she shouldn't be blamed. Because Joey always does this. Two minutes ago he would have split that kid's head with a piece of stone and now he's standing in front of me scratching his head like he's trying to decide whether he wants another beer.

He told me once, a long time ago, that he thought it was a mistake that he had lived so long. Like Fate had forgotten to cut his string.

I don't think he ever got past that notion.

Chapter 5

After the fight, I ask Joey where Terran is, and without a word he leads the way, back down the hall, his back straight, his eyes ahead. People are standing on the sidelines, watching him furtively, watching us as we pass—this strange, bloody procession. He tells them all with his countenance that his violence needs no justification.

We find her in a room, not alone exactly, if you can count the two passed out people, one by the bed, the other wedged almost impossibly behind the door. She's sitting, her back against the headboard, and when she sees us her face lights up like New Year's. She throws her arms around Joey as he leans over her; his embrace leaves red streaks across her forearms. It's disturbing, the sight of her, grinning into that face full of blood. She looks insane.

"What happened?" I ask him.

He starts to talk and then stops, his arms wrapped around her. He doesn't really need to say anything, because we can all guess—the kid made some kind of a pass at Terran, who was in no condition to refuse. Maybe he was even dumb enough to insult her. It doesn't matter. Any explanation would seem stupid now in the aftermath.

Brandon hasn't said a word. He's just standing, watching, like I usually do, and it feels strange to be the one to turn to him and say, "We need to get out of here."

We load Terran up into her SUV. It's still dark, and I'm dreading trying to inch my way out of the tangle of cars, some half-submerged in the shrubbery, their $80,000 price tags forgotten for the promise of beer. Brandon will drive Joey's Mitsubishi. Joey puts his hand through the driver's side window and links hands with me briefly without looking up. He won't talk to me about this. He won't talk to Terran either. And if he talks to Brandon, what he says will most likely be lies. But he'll be okay. When I see him next the blood will be gone. He'll be clean.

Terran's humming a nameless tune beside me. She's still high, with no sense of time or consequence. I glance at her in the dim light. Her head is rolling against the seat and she wears a small smile as her fingers weave lazy patterns in the dark. If I felt frustrated with her before, for being high, for causing trouble and still being blameless, I can't remember it now. She tells me that she loves me and takes my hand. I give her a quick squeeze and then focus on the SUV, on getting its behemoth frame past a well-camouflaged BMW. It doesn't go well. I have to back up and start over. When Terran takes my hand from the wheel again I tell her to stop.

"Are you mad?"

"No. I'm driving."

"You're mad," she says, lighting a cigarette. Her roll is getting more erratic; the low points following the highs with greater frequency. She'll be done soon. She'll talk about it tomorrow. It was good, and she'll want more. Who wouldn't want more? All that happiness guaranteed. But then I see her face, so peaceful in front of a Joey covered in gore, and think maybe not. She's like The Happy Man in that poem we studied in high school. Happy to the point of misery. To the point of delirium.

"I didn't sleep with Joey, if that's what you're mad about."

"Why would you think I would be mad about that?" I say, though I can't imagine it, her with Joey. The change is beyond comprehension. Besides, she's always been the one to stop it. She's the roadblock, not me. If she wanted Joey, there'd be nothing I could say to deter her, no emotional plea, and no practicalities. She'd take him, and that would be the end of it.

Her head lolls against the seat. "I mean, what would my mother say? Me. Screwing Joey. Marrying Joey. Can you imagine?" She's giggling because she can't not giggle. She leans over and rests her head on my shoulder, exhausted finally. "I hate my mother," she mumbles.

"I hate your mother too," I say, and then think quickly that I don't hate mine, although maybe I would, if I knew her.

I've made it out of the driveway, and the road is the four-a.m.-road, open, with deep ditches on either side. I wonder how hard I would have to jerk the wheel to send us off the edge of one. I wonder if we'd be killed on impact or if we would linger bleeding in the dark.

Terran's quiet for the rest of the drive home and nearly unconscious when I smuggle her up the stairs to my bedroom, where I will play the good friend and tuck her into my bed. I know that when I wake before her she'll look amazingly alive against the gray of my sheets, all golden hair and peach skin.

When I go down the hall to get linens and an extra pillow for myself, I have to pass my mother's room. I can hear her inside, without my father, doing her drunken crying thing like she sometimes does, and for a minute I'm mad at her. I'm mad at her broken socialite body and mad at her for the thousand times she's told me about her liberal arts degree and why degrees are important when she's never used hers for anything as far as

I can tell. She arranges banquets and parties and sits on committees. She tends the house and drinks brandy like Kool-Aid. All of these things she does more for my father than for herself. Tomorrow she'll pound mimosas and turn the ringer to the phone off until noon. She'll think desperate thoughts about what my father wants for dinner. She'll do her own shopping at the farmer's market, looking fresh, and pressed, with sunglasses on to keep from wincing at the daylight and to keep people from seeing her bloodshot eyes.

I don't know who she is. I'm standing out here with my arms full of linens and hearing her cry. I saw a picture of her once when she was in college. She was blushing and beautiful; she had books in her arms and her ebony hair was in a ponytail. That girl is my mother, I think wickedly, not that woman in there crying. Not that woman who evicted me from the womb a month early so that she could start drinking.

I'm angry with her, and with me, because I know that a lovely, blushing girl wouldn't have made much sense as my mother. Lovely, blushing girls should have lovely, blushing daughters. And I'm angry with Terran too, although I don't know why, maybe it's just too much annoyance bleeding together.

But I'm also kind of sad. Sad because it would be too strange of me to go into my mother's bedroom and ask her why. Why are you crying? Why are you miserable? Why did you change? I'm sad because she wouldn't have an answer. When I get back into my own room and roll myself up into the sheets, I'm exhausted and sleep heavy, too tired even to daydream.

◆◆◆

Terran's awake and out of my house before I'm even out of bed. She has a brunch date with her mother and never mind the ecstasy sludge in her blood; a 5-mile run will take care of that and she'll be golden-girl perfect, ready to do flashcards. I linger for another hour or two, daydreaming about pretty things in ornate, gilded cages before going downstairs.

On the way to the kitchen I run into mother, her arms full of orange tulips from which she'll wash all the nature before stuffing them into a glass vase for table dressing. We exchange good mornings and I'm surprised by my father at the table. It's nice outside and it's a Saturday. Why isn't he golfing?

"Good morning, Violet."

"Good morning, Dad." My mother is setting down orange juice and a blueberry muffin. She asks me 'waffle or pancakes' and I don't like either so I say waffle, thinking that it's easier. It turns out it doesn't matter; they've eaten both hours before and it's just a reheat on a plate with cold syrup.

But before I can even begin to ignore the saliva-like sweetness, my father sets a small stack of leaflets on the table. I pick them up and glance through them. Pamphlets and flyers and course outlines, summer studies that he's somehow managed to pilfer from my college. "In case you need something to keep you busy this summer," he says when I look up.

"Thanks, Dad," I say before cutting into my breakfast, but the look on my face must not be the right one, because his paper folds shut.

"It's just an idea."

"I know." I respond. It's very quiet except for the sound of my mother humming. "I just wanted to relax this summer. I continued" He smiles, but it's not real.

"What do you need to relax for?" He snaps. "You did thirty-thousand dollars worth of relaxing this year."

I don't say anything. Can I really argue with that? After all, I did take bowling. And all of my other courses had the words "introduction to" stamped before their titles. I know he's only worried. Worried that he doesn't know what I want and worried because he gets the distinct feeling that I don't know what I want either. But I'm fairly sure that if I told him what I wanted,

I couldn't articulate it in a way that he'd understand. These concepts are passed back and forth between us in the air as we watch each other with pursed lips. Then he smiles at me, fondly though clearly frustrated, and the newspaper goes back up.

"You know I'd go a little bit easier on you if you'd just show some initiative, Violet. You're eighteen and one year of college has gone. The world is going to grind on, with or without you in it. There's no putting it off."

I bite down hard on a square of cold, yellow sponge. Now is not the right time to tell him that I wouldn't mind being left behind.

◆◆◆

Terran picks me up a few hours later on the way to meet Joey at the gorge. I ask her how her brunch with her mother went.

"We didn't go. She canceled on me."

"That's polite."

"She canceled because she hasn't seen my grade report yet. I told her it doesn't come out for another two weeks, but she knows something's up."

I can't believe all this fuss over one B-plus. Terran pulls into the washout. Joey's Mitsubishi is already there, he'll be sitting among our sandy boulders a quarter mile up, throwing things into the stream and waiting like always. When we come around the bend he waves, Terran waves back; we leave the manmade path of stone and walk through the grass, then heave ourselves up on the rocks.

Brandon is with him, and we nod to each other. They both have beer cans in their hands and I can see more kept cool in the shade. It's kind of disgusting. I wonder if they ever really stopped drinking from the night before; they're still in the same clothes. Although the blood is gone from Joey's face and hands. Maybe he washed in the stream before we got there, leaving a red cloud and attracting the fish.

There's a fruit-basket-upset as we get on the rocks. Terran squeezes in beside Joey and I hop up behind them. Brandon ends up ousted and goes to the riverbed, walking along the edges of pale sedimentary rock, which has leached dry in patches since the last rain.

"You haven't been home," I say to Joey, and he shakes his head, which is unmarked. There isn't a single bruise or a scratch from that boy whose blood he wore.

"Would've given my mom a heart attack. Not that it would have been the first time."

"Then why did you do it?" I ask, his smile is not regretful.

"What else is there to do?" he says, "He'll live."

He will live of course. It was nothing more than a quarter pint lost. But still, something in that kid might have been broken, maybe something fundamental after being beaten in front of all those people, and Joey, with his fighting, has started spreading wrath like some kind of twisted Johnny Appleseed. When he's angry, he's angry at everything. Maybe once he was angry for a cause, but now anger itself is the cause; he's become the Anti-incarnate, and I daydream on his face for a moment. I see a man with blades protruding from his forearms, running through a crowd, blood flying like water-spray from a whale's blowhole. I know that last night he would have hit me, had I gotten in the way, and then called me stupid for interfering as an apology.

He reaches out and strokes my hair. I smile in spite of myself. Joey is what he is and maybe it doesn't matter because the world made him that way, or he has a chemical imbalance, or his mother didn't breastfeed. Maybe he's right, and it is a mistake that he's lived this long. Maybe it's a mistake that he's alive now at all. He's better suited for a world with glory, a world of aristocrats—someplace besides here, where we're all kids of parents who've made too much money, and suddenly a father's hope that his son will grow to do better than him seems like an outlandish expectation.

Terran is leaning her head on his shoulder, a small comfort. I watch them, beautiful and curled up in each other, Venus and Adonis.

Down by the water, Brandon is laughing and calling my name, so I slide off the rock to let Terran and Joey whisper in peace. Brandon is kneeling out on the rock bed, staring down at the craters formed by eddies of water that became drills over time, and smiling. When I get to him he takes my hand and pulls me down too.

The rain has flooded the stream and dried away, but not before hatching wriggling creatures and leaving them stranded in the crater pools. Minnows are straining at the edges in herds, in a panic as their puddle evaporates in the midday sun. For a minute I think that he's sick for chuckling at this tragic spectacle, and then I watch, as one tiny, wriggling body zips free of the water, skating on its little scaly belly, straight into the next crater pool, and closer to the liberating stream.

"Kamikaze minnows," he says to me, as another fish follows the first.

"What are you looking at? Terran asks from right behind me I jump. She watches, with Joey beside her, as one by one, the minnows vacate their prison, sliding along from puddle to puddle on their way to the stream.

"How do they know where they're going?" I ask.

"Brave little shits," says Joey.

"They must be able to sense it," Terran says with some finality.

"I don't think they do," says Brandon, still watching the show. "I think they just go, because they have to, because otherwise they'll just die in the puddle."

For some reason I think of the September 11th footage—that last tower falling. I think of tiny, dark bodies flying from the windows. I say as much, and Terran looks at me horrified that I should relate those people to these fish.

"Would you rather jump or be crushed?" I ask. Brandon says jump. Joey says it doesn't matter, you're dead anyway. Terran says it's a stupid question.

"September 11th is our Kennedy assassination," Brandon says, tossing a rock into the water. Terran asks him what he means, and he tells us about his eldest aunt, who, when asked about the Kennedy assassination, can recount that she was walking down the sidewalk eating a strawberry ice cream cone, talking to her friend Judy about an upcoming dance, when she heard the news. "Almost forty years later, and she can remember all that, when she can't remember if she put on underwear, most days. It'll be like that for us, too. It's the marker in our generation."

Terran is smiling. "That's true. I remember that I was studying in the library—Chapter 4 in U.S. History before 1860, and I looked up, and there were a bunch of people standing outside the window, holding hands in this big circle. I can even remember," she grins, "I can even remember a smell—someone was eating one of those greasy breakfast sandwiches from the cafeteria."

I can remember too, that I was walking in late to class and the hallways were full of people, talking very animatedly and looking nervous or excited. There was a girl in a very nice black suit saying that her father had called her to let her know that he was okay, and I remember wondering why there were twenty people standing around listening to her say so.

But I don't know if these details will stay, ready to be called up instantly like the strawberry ice cream of Brandon's aunt's girlhood. It was important yes, and we remember it, but it wasn't that long ago. I'm not so sure that Terran's breakfast sandwich smell will stand up to forty years of time. She's not Brandon's aunt. I'm not Brandon's aunt. Now is not then, and free love has unexpectedly impregnated everyone with apathy. The shrug is the new peace sign.

We're back on the rocks again, and Terran's talking idly about her mother. After a few minutes Brandon's had enough. He's back down to the streambed, looking for more kamikaze fish. Terran keeps talking to Joey, and to me, talking tough with fear in her voice, but funny, and we laugh in places.

Then, I stop listening. I watch us in our little circle and I'm back at the breakfast table of this morning. I remember my father's words about the world grinding on and I can hear it suddenly, tick tick ticking just beyond the trees. It's a carousel horse running on an already spinning carousel, all blurry lights and jointed legs, while the three of us sit on rocks and talk about the bravery of minnows.

Chapter 6

SITTING IN THE DRAWING ROOM WITH MY PARENTS AFTER A SHOWER, I JUST know that my mother's wondering whether I'm leaving a wet mark on the sofa. I probably am. My hair hanging down like seaweed has already stained the gray of my robe to black in places, and later my mother will worry at the brocade of the cushions with a chenille towel, her forehead knitted with concern. I wonder if she has any thoughts anymore that don't involve the words 'clean,' or 'orderly' or 'menu planner.' Then I remember her gin-soaked crying and I'm sorry. I pull my hair over my shoulder and wring it out with my water-logged fingertips. A big black spot expands on my chest like a wound.

My parents are sitting in adjacent chairs and they've put their book and magazine down to watch the news. It's just the local news, the second-rate news, my father calls it, behind Bloomberg and CNN I suppose. There's a moment of stillness as the anchor glances down at sheets of paper, changing her face from being delighted about recounting the adventures of Bongo the candy-striping dog to something somber, stretching down the corners of her mouth and putting on her troubled eyes.

She looks back into the camera, and my parents listen with horror and perked ears to the kind of violent event that can really pull you in and make you pay attention. I watch the grimaces and shaking heads of good people as they hear about someone shot—someone run down on 3rd and Lexington.

I sit perfectly still on the end of the sofa, and I don't feel guilty about my lack of feeling. I feel defiant. Desensitization is inevitable. It takes more than a shooting now to make me wince. I need something more awful, someone shot ten times maybe, or a strangulation victim with 3-inch deep rope burns, to make me ponder the rage it took. In five years, maybe it will take a skinning. Eventually, humanity will slip its conscience entirely, like a musty snakeskin.

◆◆◆

Tonight we're at a club and it's the perfect place. Today was too idle and full of daydreams and for once reality is refreshing. So here's this room, two floors of manic, pounding bodies and glow sticks like a rave, flashes of strobe and too much salty air, the bass beating into your skin. Sensory overload in blue. It makes it impossible to think, impossible to be anywhere but here.

Terran and I have wristbands affixed. We had no problems at the door; our fakes are good, obtained from the fat kid who lives in the dorm room at the end of Curran Hall, whose only claim to fame and acceptance is his ability to make good fakes. Terran's leading the way to the bar and the crowd parts as if they were the Red Sea and she were holding a large wooden staff.

There's never a wait for a bartender when Terran's out front; blondes get catered to and that's a perk. They get called stupid too and that's the price. In two minutes she's gotten the boys beers and herself a Cosmo, me a rum and coke and then we're off again, my fingers through the belt loops of her jeans and Joey's through mine and we're not three people anymore, but a three-jointed creature, like those paper dragons in Chinese parades.

We sit and the bass pounds, reminding my heart to beat. I think I could stay here forever, watching the bodies' rhythmic stomp and twist, sometimes so uniform it's like watching machines in a factory. Brandon drags me out onto the floor, and we dance. He barely touches me. He doesn't dance like other boys, so close with their arms around you, trying to grind in to get their crotch against your crotch or your ass.

It's hot, my drink is gone already, soaking into the lining of my empty stomach too fast. By the end of the night I might have the spins from my too-tainted blood and the sweat of other people. I'm dying of thirst so I leave Brandon with some relief; we were surrounded by three or four girls trying to attract his attention, their not-so-subtle gyrations meant to tell him that they'd be perfectly willing to join him out back among the used condoms.

At the bar I wait, because I'm not blonde, and there's a girl next to me with a very tiny tank top on, the word "Feminist" printed in large block letters right across the boobs. She has got her back to the bar, staring very hard at something, and since no one's coming to take my order I turn around and look where she's looking.

She's watching Terran, dancing on the second floor, blonde hair flying. She dances like she's had training, which she hasn't; it's just another natural talent to hate her for. Next to her, almost on top of her, and not really dancing at all is Joey. They look right together, so well-matched on the outside. Walking down the street they'd never get the puzzled glances that come of seeing a very pretty girl with an average boy, or the pronounced double-takes that come of seeing a pretty boy with an ugly girl. I look at the feminist beside me, and there's real disdain for the two people sweating up there, real disdain in the curl of her black-lined pierced lip. There is hungry envy in her eyes as well, and I think that the hunger might be for Terran and the envy might be for Joey, but then again maybe it's just her ironic tank top that makes me think so.

It's taken so long to get a bartender that when I do I order two rum and cokes plus a shot, any shot, whatever the guy feels like making. He shakes up something creamy and chocolate-sweet, but I didn't specify so I take it and pay and go back to the table. Brandon has no more need of me on the dance floor; he's got a girl on each side doing the grind on his leg and he's got an arm around each. They're both blonde, slithering like snakes, their shimmering halter tops covered with sequin-scales. I wonder if he perceives the danger, to be the object of such lust, that each girl could unhinge her jaw suddenly and devour him in a few wrenching bites.

Across the neon flash I can see Terran and Joey, no longer dancing. They're standing, leaning against the wall, talking very close and very serious. They've each got a hand on each other, hers against his chest and his on her hip. I wonder why they haven't come back to the table. I wonder what they must be talking about, and I watch them, willing them to look up and smile, wave and make their way over. But there's nothing but nodding heads and moving lips. I should be there listening too, completing my normal point on the triangle. I suddenly feel really stupid and mad, sitting here alone. When Brandon asks me if I need another drink I don't answer. I blame him, even though there isn't any logic in it. I blame him because I've somehow been delegated to be the host to this tourist, even though he's Joey's cousin, not mine. So I am with him and that leaves them, because they would never consider forming a square. And they're taking advantage of it.

"I didn't mean to leave you out there."

He's close enough to my ear that I can smell the beer on his breath. I shut my eyes and swivel them to the left so that when I open them again it's Brandon that I see instead of Terran and Joey intertwining fingers.

"What?"

He jerks his head toward the dance floor. "Out there. I didn't mean to ditch out on you. Those girls were just—." He pauses here and bows his head like a sorry hound dog, looking up at me through the hair that has fallen into his eyes. He's so pretty I can barely stand it, but even as he's apologizing to me, he glances sidelong at a girl who is smiling at him from another table. Smiling and nibbling on her fingertip. He tries not to smile back but can't quite manage the suppression.

I sigh and he apologizes again, grinning this time and more sincere, but I shake my head.

"It doesn't matter," I say. "Really. Do what you want. Do you want to dance with Little Miss Delicious Phalanges over there?"

He laughs at me. I know that I sound sarcastic, but I'm serious. He's rejecting me, sure. He's underwhelmed by my mousy hair and dollar-bill eyes, and who can blame him? He wants what all the boys want: a flashy, sexy, bubbly girl who is sweet and smart and...and...and nothing. That package should be enough for anybody. And I am not that package. I'm the anti-package. He's looking at me really pitifully. It's pissing me off.

"Listen," I half-shout over the bass, "Don't worry about it. Stop looking at me with that guilty expression." When he doesn't, I snap, "Knock it off. I'm immune to disappointment."

"That's impossible. How can someone be immune to disappointment?"

"Easy. Don't hope for anything." We blink at each other. I had meant that to be flippant, but the moment I said it I was somehow sad, and so was he. I looked away first.

"I knew you in the coffee shop."

Even though I suspected that he did, I ask, "How?"

"Joey talks about you all the time. And he showed me pictures once, your school pictures, yours and Terran's."

"Why didn't you say anything?"

He shrugs. "It was more interesting not to."

◆◆◆

Middle of the day and Terran and I are at the mall, in a department store, Bloomingdales maybe, I don't know. We've been through too many already, and the mall is filled with women attacking the spring sales with military fervor. They knock into each other and rifle through piles of previously well-folded clothing, hunting for a size, a color, something to make them feel prettier, or thriftier. Any new thing to infuse into an old life. I bump into a woman with sunglasses perched atop her head and mumble an apology; she looks at me with condescension. Years of spring sales have taught her that "excuse me's" are for the weak.

We're standing in line for the fitting rooms, both of our arms loaded down with Terran's choices. The lines are so long that they weave back in a serpentine through the merchandise racks. We're ushered up closer, with quick snippets of conversation to ascertain our well-being, "Did you find everything all right?" "Was anyone helping you today?" This only adds to the overall confusion. I feel like I'm about to be frisked at an airport security check.

When it's Terran's turn I don't go in with her; I've always thought that was weird when she can just change and come out for me to see. But this time I should have, because she doesn't come out, and doesn't say anything while she's inside, trying on four suits of conservative color. I picture her in there, staring at herself, a lovely, living mannequin, but there's no smile on her face, because this is her mother's shopping trip. She's got her mother's platinum card in her purse. Terran doesn't shop for suits.

When she picked me up this morning, her shoulders were too straight, we weren't 5 miles down the road before she turned down the radio and said, "My mom got me an internship."

I don't ask where, where else but Meredith's firm, where she can be watched and reported on. She told me that she starts June 1st and I remembered something she said to me once, driving to or from a party—that I should get my own car.

"What kind of adult doesn't have their own car? Most kids are itching for one the minute they turn 16. Don't tell me your parents wouldn't buy you one."

"Of course my parents would," I said, "but what do I need a car for, when I've got you to haul me around." I remembered that, and for a minute felt stupid for becoming so dependent on one person. That feeling comes back again and I shake that selfishness off; her summer is over and I'm wondering how I'm going to get downtown and back. I'm wondering what I'm going to do without her and how my days will pass.

She's taking a long time and I start to worry. I imagine her never coming out. I see her bricking herself up in that tiny pink room with the ridiculous striped bench, calmly smoothing the mortar, laying down the stones and looking into her mother's face in the mirror. I walk up and knock, say "Hey, how's it going," and the door opens on "going" so the word only peters out of my mouth.

And there's nothing wrong. She's fine, the jackets and skirts are back on their respective hangers and she brushes past me with all of them. I had let my daydream get the best of me—one more tick on the Violet stupidity scale. "They all fit," she says flatly, and I don't say that I wish I had that problem, because then she would hate me for not understanding her disappointment.

◆◆◆

There's a party at Julia's, which we get to at about 10:30. There are always more girls than guys at Julia's parties, which usually ends up being some kind of bad situation, Terran's been drinking hard since seven to prep for it. I don't blame her. When she walks through the door every girl there will size her up, compare her to the others and to themselves, and will find themselves wanting. Most of them will hate her, just for that. We're malicious, manipulative, narcissistic things, girls, maybe because there are fewer men than women, maybe because it's in our nature. Maybe because men have lied and cheated since the beginning of time and succeeded in pitting us against each other. It doesn't matter. It's a dynamic we can't escape from, and any woman who manages to transcend it will probably end up alone. It makes me want to be a man sometimes, so if nothing else I could sleep with a lot of people and be called a stud instead of a slut.

Terran and Julia are sharing a brief hug. She's drunk and Julia isn't—playing responsible hostess. I bristle at the disadvantage. Julia welcomes me too, there's a flicker of distaste for Joey, she probably remembers his face smeared in blood.

Most of the people are gathered around Julia's long oak dining table, playing some drinking game or another; Ride the Train, Circle of Death, Screw the Dealer—names that clearly identify their potential harm and which only serve to make them more enticing. Terran still gets the stares and squints as she approaches, but the hate has been softened by Brandon because now they can measure our group as an acceptable trade: one gorgeous girl and two hot guys.

Cups in hand, we sit and join in. Terran lasts two hours before she starts to tire and goes off up the stairs; I last another half before I go to find her. Joey and Brandon hardly notice; they're really drunk—the whole table is really drunk, and the conversation has gotten dumber not even a month back from college. No more politics and theorem analysis. It's been replaced by a lot of breast-flashing and yelling.

Before I make it to the stairs I pass a bathroom. The door is open. I can hear giggling—malicious, manipulative, narcissistic giggling. There are at least three of them in there—the stereotypical group—and what do they do in there that they all need to go together? Do they each pee in quick succession, like human versions of those assembly line machines that fill soda bottles?

I know that the giggles are about Terran before they even say her name, so I listen as they take her down and build themselves up. They have to because her beauty has stolen their identities. They are less now than they were before she arrived.

But after five minutes, I'm still pissed off and bored all at once so I walk over to the bathroom door and slam it on them hard, hoping for fingers but finding none. At least I know that when the door creeps open, there won't be anything for Julia's surprised eyes to see but my fading back going up the stairs. When I find Terran, she's sitting alone in a dark guest bedroom, sitting on the bed and facing the windows.

"You drunk?" I ask.

"Before we even got here," she says. She turns, and I can't see her expression in the shadows. "Come on in, you'd better catch up." She holds out a cup and I take it, then stand next to her and drink while she stares out the windows again.

"They're talking about you downstairs," I say. I don't need to tell her what they're saying, or who's saying it, but I do anyway.

"She says I'm conceited?" Terran says, incredulous, even though lots of people say that about her. I nod and lean down, noticing for the first time a pendant swaying against her neck. I pick it up between my fingers, try to look at it in the moonlight.

"Conceit is a lie, Violet, you know that don't you?" she says without slurring.

"Don't pay attention to Julia; she's two-faced to everyone, if you haven't noticed."

Terran waves me off, a little of her drink sloshing onto the coverlet.

"Julia doesn't matter any more than any other bitch." She laughs, still not looking at me. "I'm talking about conceit. I'm not conceited."

"I know you're not."

"I'm not because it would be stupid. Nobody can be any better or any worse than anyone else, except in these small ridiculous circles, and what does that matter?" I ask her what she means. "I mean that with so many people walking around it'd be naïve to assume that there aren't hundreds or thousands or millions of people who are better than you at everything that you're good at. So what if I'm pretty, or if I'm smart. There's always going to be someone prettier and smarter."

"Well I'm never going to meet them," I say, and she shakes her head, puffs on a joint that I hadn't noticed, and then rolls it between her fingers. She lets it burn without offering me any.

"It's the same with love, you know," she says. "None of the people we love are any better than the hundreds of thousands of others we could love just as much. Soul mates are lies we tell ourselves. Nobody's special." She makes a rumbling, exhaling sound, a laugh with no humor. She adds in a sad voice. "Makes everything seem kind of over dramatic, doesn't it?"

It's almost incomprehensible to me that someone like her could feel this way, that someone who is envied by everyone I know just said the words of someone trapped in the middle. But I sit down beside her and feel the bed sink, feel the weight pressing in, the force of a world so crowded that we have to squeeze by, shoulder-to-similar-shoulder. With so many lives living, and so many brains teeming, it's difficult to believe that anyone ever has an original thought.

She slips her fingers into mine and falls back onto the pillows. I can hear the gem of her pendant fall down its chain. It sounds like someone rappelling down a wire behind me in the dark. Then it hits bottom and thumps onto satin, and I keep staring out the windows, holding her hand, and we ignore the voices of our friends downstairs, that have mingled together to form one noise that we can't recognize.

◆◆◆

On the first day of Terran's internship, I'm in the backyard. It's so quiet, and I'm hopeful; I think that if there's clarity coming to me it'll be here, where the fog becomes dew on the opening petals of my mother's lilies. I have no luck. There's no moment of realization where I can see forward, or even backward, and even my attempt doesn't last long. I'm not suited for meditation. Zen will always escape me, because the space between my ears braids itself into daydreams too quickly. Then there's just my body, lying in the gazebo with its eyes open, like the abandoned shell of an idiot.

When Brandon comes around the corner and says "hi," I almost groan. I had just gotten to the good part of the daydream—the coliseum screaming and the lion at my throat. I haven't spoken out loud for hours, the sun is going down, so I can come back to the lions later, fast-forward or rewind, edit and splice. Daydreams are better than movies.

He sits across from me and I ask him what he's doing here. He tells me that Terran's at Joey's house, he doesn't know how I can stand to be the third plane in that triangle; they drove him out in ten minutes with all of their touching and whispers. The information blows away the last of the coliseum dust. She has gone to Joey to be comforted after her first day, but if she were smart she'd have come to me, because we could laugh and eat and I'd listen without asking to mess around afterward. I want to tell Brandon that it's his fault—that it was never like this before he came. That the three of us moved in a consistent pattern, from one to the other and back to Terran, and it'd still be that way if he hadn't come. Even as I think that, my brain beats it down. Because it really started that day in the car, that day she told Joey what she hadn't told me, before I ever met Brandon, and if he weren't here, I'd have probably daydreamed the day away and slept out here in the gazebo only to wake up in the morning and do it again.

He's sitting there, looking at me without accusations. I feel stupid lying on my back with my knees up and also kind of guilty, so I say, "Let's go to the gorge."

The river is up again and the minnows are gone, escaped into the stream to become bigger fish. Even so, Brandon's scouring the shorelines for them, wanting to see them victorious in the open water.

"Clarity again, weren't you?" I blink. I hadn't been listening and only just now realize that I've been perched on the rock not moving, not moving for so long that I've become a stone gargoyle, and at any minute a gout of rainwater and pigeon-shit could spray from my mouth. Gross.

"What?"

"I said, you were looking for clarity again, weren't you? Out in the garden. Trying to force an epiphany."

I shrug. "I guess so." He shakes his hand dry, kneeling by the bank. "Honestly Violet, I don't think you'd know what to do with it if you found it. Besides, you'll probably give yourself a nosebleed."

"What's that supposed to mean?" He laughs and tells me not to get offended. He says that he likes me this way, always looking for something, as though being defined by an effort has more value than being defined by an accomplishment.

A great, irrational feeling of gladness that he's here makes me hop off of the rock and walk down to his side, where he's taking off his shoes and socks to wade in the stream. I follow along, hopping on stones and he holds my hand to steady me. If he were Joey, he'd shove me into the water and then pull me back out and hug me to his chest, laughing the whole time while I sputtered. Terran would slap him on the shoulder when we got back to the bank, then take me under her arm and laugh too.

"Brandon, can I ask you a stupid question?"

"There aren't any stupid questions."

"That's just something that stupid teachers say," I fire back, oh so clever, and he smiles and nods, but I hesitate despite the invitation. How many conversations have started off like this, with the permission to ask any one of a multitude of idiotic or inappropriate things? I could go anywhere with it; maybe I didn't have a question in mind in the first place. "What do you want to be? I mean, ultimately?"

"Ultimately? Like, in the end? Or like, in the full of my potential?" I shrug. And to think that I could have asked him anything. What's the difference between a bullfrog and a toad? Were you a bed wetter? How many girls have you been with and do you think you're a slut? But I didn't ask him any of those things, and he's found an answer already. He says, "Well, someday it'd be nice to be discussed in intelligent circles. And to be referred to by my last name only."

"That's not an answer," I smile. He shrugs to signify that it sounded like one to him. And I suppose that it is. I picture nine intellectuals gathered around a wooden table, bottles of wine and discarded glasses littered along its surface, using his name to give weight to their own thoughts, calling themselves intelligent because they have heard him, have read him, have interpreted what he had to say. Brandon seeks his immortality in the minds of other people.

"What about you, Violet? What are you going to be?"

"My father says I should be a doctor."

"Is that why you told me you were a Med student?"

"He says it'll make me a good person. Except that I don't know if he means 'good' exactly. Maybe he just means 'worthwhile.' That's the clarity I'm looking for, an epiphany of a way to become worthwhile, a way that I can stand."

Brandon says that it's impossible to place a value on a person and asks me what I want. What I want.

How can I tell him that I don't want anything? Not my father's life, not my mother's, not even mine, just the world that's in my head. So I purse my lips on my words. "I don't know what I want. Doesn't it seem like everything's boring, after a while? I don't know how people do it. These careers that last for fifty years. These lives that last for fifty years."

We turn and he walks me back across the stream. "A man works as an air traffic controller 5 days a week," he says. "Every day he rides the bus home from the same stop. On Thursdays he eats meatloaf. Does laundry on Sunday. What do you call his life?"

"Mundane," I say without missing a beat.

"What do you call it if he's happy?" He wades out of the water and stands beside me. He's trying to tell me that there's nothing in the world that isn't perception and perspective, telling me via analogy to keep the message from becoming rhetoric on a billboard. Life is what you make of it. Home is where the heart is. Got Milk? It's all spin. We watch the water going by and I tell him that perception can't be understood; it can't be quantified. We're all stuck in our own little realities, the realities of our own heads. Only during a game of musical lives could we ever really know what's real.

"Maybe none of this is real," he muses. "Maybe we're all just characters in a nonstop movie that's playing in another dimension."

I shove him with my shoulder and realize with a twinge that I've missed doing that to Terran.

"Don't be ridiculous. How could anyone watch a movie that's this artless?" He smiles and catches me around the shoulders with his arm.

"Life's not artless. It just feels that way because we can't hear the soundtrack."

On the way back to the car we hold hands, and I don't blame him for anything anymore. I'm just glad that he's taking me on the scenic route, away from the usual path and through the weeds, poison ivy be damned. We come out at another part of the river, and I see Joey's car parked on the opposite bank and they're both sitting on the trunk.

Brandon raises his hand to his mouth, ready to call out but I stop him with a hand on his chest. They're moving closer to each other now, reaching, and they're kissing, and it's not a kiss of friendship, and not the dead kiss that Joey gave to me the night we came home, but one of tongues and hands and lust and importance. I stand and watch them, and Brandon watches me, watches my irises fill up with the bodies of my friends.

I suppose I should have expected this. It must have been so obvious to everyone else. But it wasn't to me. Not after watching Terran dance around his advances for all these years. But there they are. Kissing madly like old Hollywood royalty. Bogart and Bacall. Hepburn and Tracy. But if there's music playing in another dimension, it's not an instrumental piece, let me tell you.

Chapter 7

My father insists that I meet him for breakfast on Thursday, downtown in a little diner, eight o'clock sharp—the time set to compel me to wake up early. I walk in at five minutes past and he frowns; he's probably been sitting there since 7:20 tapping his watch.

"Hi, Dad," I say and the waitress hands me a menu in fingerprinted plastic. The diner is something out of the fifties, but the retro-feel isn't intentional; it's just that it hasn't been updated since then.

"Good morning, Violet. Trouble getting a cab?"

"Mom dropped me off."

"Oh." He doesn't ask why she hasn't come in to join us. Instead he talks in a very important voice while I look over the menu, about deals and clients and I get the impression that I'm supposed to be grateful that he's with me this morning instead of with them. Or maybe I'm being unfair and he's saying these things to make me feel loved, to imply that I'm more important.

We order eggs and pancakes, and my father flirts with the waitress a little. After she leaves, smiling over her shoulder, I ask him how life at the office is, and the topic carries us through our juice. I can't tell whether or not he really likes his job, but there are certainly things that he likes about it, he's a partner in a financial consulting firm and it affords him many perks: six figure salary, country club membership, leisurely eight o'clock breakfast with his wayward daughter.

"So your mother tells me that your friend Terran got herself an internship at her mother's firm."

I eyeball him over my juice, wondering why they were talking about Terran, and whether I can tell my mother anything without it being like a note passed to my father. Thankfully the food arrives, and it gives me a minute to collect myself while we spread butter and jam.

"Yeah, she's in the finance department, I think."

He's nodding as he salts his eggs. "She's a very put together girl. She's always been at the top of her class. She's at the top again at college, isn't she?"

I nod, stuff pancake into my mouth dry, willing myself to choke, but damn it, I swallow and he goes on.

"It's good that you're friends with her, Violet. It's always a pleasure to have her at the house. She's so energetic, and just lovely. Honestly, if you had to follow someone to school, I'm glad that it was her. How are your pancakes?"

"Fine," I say. He's done this before, measured us against each other, like she's not my friend but my big sister. He's done it periodically since it became obvious who would come out on top. It's never bothered me before. After all, I know that she outdoes me in nearly everything. But she doesn't care, so I can love her because of it instead of envy her, only this time I'm annoyed, so when he asks how she likes her internship, I say:

"I don't know. I haven't seen very much of her since she started seeing Joey."

"Oh," he says, and some of the approval leaves his voice. Like Meredith, and practically every other adult, he's never liked Joey. I'm glad to take the weight out of his lungs. Before I know it I'm telling him how Brandon and I saw them kissing at the river without them knowing. Leaking it to him makes me breathe easier, my little revenge for her not telling me after so many days. But maybe there's nothing to tell. Maybe what I saw really was just a kiss, and she decided not to take it any further. Maybe it was just like Joey and me, on my bed, the night we came home.

"Who's Brandon?"

"What?"

He says it again, and the name is probably the only thing that he retained from my outburst. I should be glad. Because what kind of friend am I to betray her to my father? I tell him that Brandon is Joey's cousin. In the future he'll keep his ears open for that name, maybe because he heard my voice change when I said it.

Breakfast is over. Now he'll pay the bill and head to the office; I'll probably hang around downtown for a while and then take a cab home. Before he goes, he says to me, "You know, Violet, if you ever want an internship, all you have to do is ask."

I smile at him and give him a hug and quick kiss, then wave at him as he steps off the curb. Terran said once that it isn't nepotism if you deserve it. With me, it'd definitely be nepotism.

◆◆◆

On Saturday, Terran shows up unexpectedly at my house. I hear her talking to my mother and leave my room to lean over the railing; she sees me and smiles. There's something nervous in it, something reluctant. That smile tells me she's finally going to tell me about Joey—that smile tells me there really is something to tell.

She has prepared for it, rehearsed it, her speech is determined and obvious, even so it takes her a while, up in my room;

she pages through one of my mother's magazines and makes it through several rounds of Six Degrees of Kevin Bacon before she lets the glossy paper slap shut and looks at me seriously. I think she looks like her mother, being so direct, and it makes me look away.

"How's the internship going?" I ask her. Despite my irritation at being left out, I'm compelled to change the subject before it even starts. I realize that I don't really want to know about her and Joey. It's better to guess and make them sneak around. The kiss is playing in a repeating reel behind my eyes and each time it becomes slightly more graphic. I think I can see a tongue. I think his hand slides up her shirt. I'd like to push these embellishments aside—to burn the whole thing. I can picture the image melting away from the center, frame by celluloid frame. If she tells me about it now, her conscience will be clear. She and Joey will be free, and I'll be obligated to accept it, and not only that, but to be happy for them, and then in the future there will be many more images to burn.

Thinking of her internship, she smiles and leans back on my pillows, her former intensity forgotten. "It's just like I thought it would be. I photocopy and sit in on meetings and look over reports that are just pretty colors. Yesterday I listened to my mother talk to one of her officers about an ex-pat with culture shock and all I'm thinking is that I wish I could read lips so that I could plug my ears there it must be a less annoying way of learning things than having to actually HEAR them."

I exhale a weak laugh. Her story doesn't affect me much; it has been diluted already—passing through Joey's ears. But I can see that she hates it. Her mother's plan is backfiring; with every minute spent at the office she knows that it's not what she wants. I hope she breaks free of Meredith with a slap. I hope that she makes her own way. I start to tell her so.

"Joey kissed me." Just like that and we're both silent. Something about the way that she said it irks me, like she's putting too much responsibility on his lips. She isn't saying anything else, just sitting there, facing me, seeming like she's looking into my face when really she's focusing on my temple. I tell her that I already know. I tell her I saw them that day at the gorge, with Brandon. There's a white flash in her eyes and for a second I feel what it's like to be up against her, the trembling punk to her Dirty Harry, and I understand why girls like Julia have to cut her down.

"You were with Brandon?" I nod, and I'm glad that I hadn't told her. My paltry little revenge.

"It took you a long time to tell me about Joey."

"We thought you'd be upset." So they've been discussing it. Discussing me. I wonder what they say about me, when I'm not there to censor their opinions.

I shrug my shoulders, and I'm struck by the realization that it's the first time I've ever had to force a shrug. "Why would you think that?"

"Because Joey told me what happened the night we came home from college."

Asshole, is what I think, but I hear my voice saying, "told you about what," in a faraway tone. I remember Joey, smiling in my doorway, swearing me to secrecy about his hands on me, about his tongue in my mouth. And now he's been the one to tell her. Still, I can't quite believe that he's forward-thinking enough to have reserved the truth for himself on purpose.

"That you kissed," she says gently, uncomfortably. I sit up.

"We didn't kiss. It was nothing. That's why I didn't tell you." She keeps going like I didn't say anything. She says that something's going on between them, that something probably has been for years. She wants to know if I'm okay with it, but that's not what she means. She means that I have to say I *am* okay with it, that I'm perfectly fine with the shift in our dynamic, never mind that it definitely has been going on for years, but only on his side. And now the only thing that has changed is she needs something from him. It's suddenly important that he feels the way that he feels about her. So often our need of another person is only linked to what that person feels about us; we're in love with what we see reflected in their eyes. We're in love with ourselves, perfected. Idealized. But I tell her it's fine, great even, and manage to hug her because that's the only acceptable answer. She's relieved and doesn't ask any more about the night that we came home from school, and she doesn't ask about Brandon. We just talk, easy, like we always have and for a few minutes everything is normal. But before long, her eyes are moving—eager to be out of here—wanting to see him. Their relationship has changed and he's been made new while I am still old and unexciting. She's thinking of him while I talk. Sometimes she throws in 'mm hmms' out of context or just blanks out on me. It pisses me off, so after a while I tell her I'm getting tired, and she springs up, finally free. Her demeanor reminds me of Joey's sometimes when he's alone with me, always wanting her. She says goodbye and tries to hide her excitement, but it hides poorly, like a fat man behind a sapling. I watch her go, angry and envious, that she doesn't want me. That she looks so alive.

◆◆◆

I'm waiting at a streetlight for the walk sign with my headphones on, Rufus Wainwright singing about cigarettes and chocolate milk, and I'm thinking about Brandon's life soundtrack, watching the lights switch. Watching the people who aren't watching me. The music is confined to the space between my ears, and that makes it entirely mine, not like music blasting from a radio or some loudspeaker in a store. It's a separate, secret thing that pulls me out of the world and lets me be the watcher from another dimension.

A bump at my shoulder makes me stumble off of the curb. There's the blast of a horn over the cheerful languid tunes in my headphones; I feel hands dragging me back up onto the sidewalk. Out of the corner of my eye I see the car pass, terribly close and terribly red, just one more of those could-have-died moments that we shrug off because they're not serious enough to warrant being called 'near-death.' But I wonder how many could-have-died moments that people have in a lifetime. If they were counted, would they average out the same? Could someone come up with an anecdote for people like they have for cats?

There is a guy in front of me mouthing something, so I shut off the music, tell him not to worry about almost killing me, and then flip it back on. Two songs later, without realizing it I've left the busy streets behind. I'm on the street where a few weeks ago I saw a man sweeping, and when my legs stop I'm in front of his deli. The door is propped open with a brick and it smells of bread and seasoned meat. I can still recall the expression on his face as he let me pass that day, something so touching in that smile from a world apart that I feel obligated to patronize his place.

When I go inside he's there, behind the counter, listening to a customer. He wears the same smile for her as he did for me, and the feeling of camaraderie instantly slips and then slips still further, because as she glances down through the glass I can see for a minute what's underneath that smile, which is plain dislike. He dislikes her so intensely that if the food were prepared behind closed doors he would spit in it.

He catches me staring and knows that I've seen. He's ashamed and a little apprehensive, like he thinks I might pull a whistle out of my pocket and blow. Then the woman is talking and he is smiling again; they are motioning their hands together, each trying to make their meanings clear. I feel awkward but I can't just walk out. There's a sudden urge to understand that dislike, to understand that shame, and to make him see that I can identify. I can't help it. It's that annoying, condescending urge to relate to something that is unrelatable. It's a pat on the hand like a stab in the throat, sweet words spoken through cracked lips. Understanding and pity look so similar. I give him my order and say nothing. There's no way to express it. My eyes don't even reach his, which are dark, chocolate brown and speak only of the challenge of being polite. It stings, ridiculously, because of course he doesn't remember me. To him I was just a passing shadow that delayed his sweeping. It's only my concept of him, my thoughts of him that give him a place in my head and make him significant. There is an inequality in the weight that people carry with each other, even among strangers.

I sit by the window and smile when he brings me my food, nodding congenially and setting it on the table, a dusting of white flour on his pink palms. His accent when he tells me to enjoy is delicate and practiced. I chew slowly to cover my ignorance. For all I know he might be from India, Morocco, or Pakistan. He might be a Buddhist, a Hindu, or a fucking Hare Krishna. But in the end, it doesn't matter. Because most people are just as ignorant as I am. And mass ignorance makes the truth irrelevant. I try not to look as he cleans up after my food behind the counter, only twenty feet away. I want to believe that his dislike of me is new, that ten months ago the smile was real. Maybe ten months ago he declared himself an American, clearly and loudly, to anyone who would listen. Maybe he loved it as his place. Then some fuckers went and used box-cutters to steer jets into buildings, so now he has to dislike it, and dislike me, an ignorant girl with headphones. There's that stupid compulsion again; I want to get up and tell him that in this at least I'm not ignorant, that I understand, because you can't ever really escape the place that you came from. The rest of the world won't allow it.

I think about Terran's mother's ex-pat and wonder where he is—think of all of the others scattered across the globe and wonder how many secretly want to shed their country. And how many stubbornly cling to it. Maybe they listen to citizens berate the United States and are left standing with their hands in their pockets, shuffling their feet and mumbling about good intentions. America feels like an unscrupulous prom queen, looking down at her broken tiara and noticing that even her friends only smile until she turns her back.

◆◆◆

"Hello?"

"Hi, is Violet there?" I know that voice, so familiar that it makes my brain itch when I can't place it. At least twenty male faces flipbook through my head: uncles, cousins, friends. Apparently I need to have two senses activated to make a match.

"Speaking," I say, and he goes on talking without an introduction which means I know him well, and that I should be embarrassed to have forgotten. It isn't until we've caught up on each other's summers that he says, "So, are you really okay with me and Katie?" and I realize that it's Brian. The guy I made Terran avoid on our way out of the school parking lot. The ex-boyfriend who cheated on me with my friend Katie Quinn. I read these facts back mentally, one after the other, acting as secretary to my own brain before assuring him that yes, I'm fine, and the relief in my voice from finally remembering who he is actually makes the response sound genuine.

"Listen, I'm coming through town next weekend to visit a friend. Do you want to have dinner on Saturday?" I vaguely wonder what sort of friend he's visiting that he'll sacrifice a night to eat with a hostile ex-girlfriend, but through my thoughts I can hear myself say yes.

◆◆◆

Brandon and I are watching the last of the day black out. We're parked at the edge of a field in his beat-up Chevy, a rust bucket car with misaligned headlights and an exhaust system that's been jimmy-rigged with wire. When he picked me up, I asked him why he keeps it and he said it reminds him of an old beagle he had growing up, one-eared and blind, that peed everywhere. The car is quiet now, shut off except for a low buzz from the radio, its gauges fading out in the trailing light. There's a full moon, and the fog lays low on the ground, lying so still and so thick that it looks solid. It's almost too beautiful, like it doesn't belong here, or like we don't belong here. Like we took a turn into this field and somehow left America.

Brandon's gotten me nicely stoned, maybe too stoned, because in the dark of the car my hands are roaming lazily across my legs like two pale, blind cave crabs. This is the sort of thing that Terran and I used to do with Joey, drive out somewhere and get fucked up, then talk until dawn. My stoned mind can't grasp how it is that they're suddenly okay without me, maybe even happier without me, like I was never necessary in the first place but just weight in the back.

"You never answered my question the last time," he says. "About what you want to be. You just told me what your father wanted you to be."

"That's because I don't know." I smile at him. He's very pretty, sitting lazy behind the wheel, all his features made soft by the blue. There is dark, shaggy hair falling across his forehead. I'd like to brush it away, so it's a good thing that my cave-crab hands have gone dead numb. "I'm eighteen and I don't know what I want to do. Nothing appeals to me more than anything else. It's infuriating, because nothing matters now except the decision."

He rolls his eyes to say 'says who?' and I glance at him sharply because it's the whole world that says so. No dragging your feet, time to become productive. Remember all that coddling and self-esteem nurturing we did for you when you were young? Well now it's time to see if that turned you into anything useful. And at 18 I'm already behind schedule.

He says, "So that's why you're chasing after clarity. You're scared of the decision. You want a sure thing."

"I'm not scared of the decision. I just don't want to wake up someday and realize that I've made the wrong choice. I'm taking my time."

"Take all the time you want. And enjoy it, because when the time comes for you to finally decide, you'll be no more certain of what you choose than you are right now."

"You don't get it," I say, and the moment it passes my lips it sounds stupid, full of childish indignation. I wish I wasn't so high, that the smoke hadn't wrapped itself around my tongue, scorched my vocal cords and rendered me inarticulate.

"Don't I? You want everything to be clear, for there to be no conflict with what you decide. No second guessing. Who wouldn't want that? It's a big burden lifted. But maybe you're right.

"Maybe I don't get it.

"People are always waiting around for someone to 'get them.'" And here he makes annoying little air quotes. "But I didn't think that you were, when didn't you just say that we're all trapped inside of our own experiences? That empathy doesn't exist? That it's impossible to 'get' anyone?"

"But it's not impossible to want," I counter. "Empathy exists in concept, if not in practice."

He reaches up and brushes my hair back off of my shoulder. It's a tender gesture, and unexpected. I realize that I just started to argue against myself.

"So," he says after his fingers trail off down my arm, "you do see that you're stuck, don't you? Choice breeds risk, which breeds uncertainty. Would you trade your will away just to save yourself an ulcer?"

I don't have an answer for that, because it's not just an ulcer that must be avoided but an ulcer of being a loser. I listen as he tells me what everyone already knows, that there are no possibilities without risk, no failure, no mistakes, no triumph. Despite that knowledge I'm very tired of this choice in front of me, and I feel very stupid for not being able to make it, when everyone else seems perfectly capable. When I look for answers I find only maybe and perhaps, infuriating little words that poke holes in control and say that there is no fate, there is no destiny. Those things went the way of the dinosaurs with King Arthur and his knights. And now the rest of us idiots are milling around in the scraps and bone, trying to construct a unicorn out of the crumbled pieces.

"I love it out here," Brandon says, looking out onto the field of fireflies with their butts blinking on and off, like little moving radio towers.

"And isn't it strange that you came to see Joey and he ditched you for a chick."

"And now I'm stuck with you," he says, and I can hear the grin in his voice. I wonder what Terran and Joey are doing now. They're undoubtedly together, being disgustingly romantic. When did I become this bitter? "Do you want to do this again next Saturday?" Brandon asks me.

I shake my head. "I can't. I have a date."

"With who?" I realize with a kick that he's jealous, and that I'm glad. I shrug. "No one important."

◆◆◆

There's only one thing to do when I get home and my father's having a drink in the sitting room, and that's go in and talk to him. I lean over the sofa and kiss him on the cheek. As I do, I get a big whiff of scotch, which means either a bad day at the office or with my mother. There are three fingers of it swirling in the tumbler in his hand, and probably a baker's dozen more in his stomach or already down the toilet.

"Late night?" he asks, and I look at the clock—that damned clock always ticking. It belonged to my mother's mother and her mother before her. What a pity that the fucker still works, but with that much history there's no throwing it out. Someday it'll tick in my house, if I ever have one. It's 1:15. I shrug when he says I keep impossible hours, that it's no wonder I can't wake up in the mornings. He's one to talk. Out of the house by 5 and home by eight, usually back in on Saturdays. Still, I've never felt neglected, and as I sit down I think that stretching his time is my father's greatest talent, although my mother, presumably upstairs and drinking on her own, might disagree.

"Fight with Mom?"

He rubs my hands between his. "You're chilly," he says and then heaves himself up to the mini bar, where he freshens his drink and brings me back a brandy. He looks his age for once, firelight hollowing out the spaces under his eyes, and the scotch making his face slack.

"Contributing to a minor," I quip. He smiles and says that I'm a young woman now, enough with all of this keg beer. I should be learning to drink like an adult. I wonder if that's wise, considering that my mother is an alcoholic.

"Fight with Mom?" I ask again, but I know that's what happened. If it were a bad day at work he wouldn't be so into bonding with me.

"Your mother," he says, passing ownership to me, which means she's being a nuisance. If she were being pleasing, he'd claim her by using her first name, "has a drinking problem."

And the cow says moo, I wanted to say, but instead we smile at the absurdity of my father, wasted on the sofa because he's upset about his wife's drinking problem. After the smiles fade, we sit for a long time. Neither of us suggests that we help her, or that she seek help on her own. Honestly, after all this time I don't know who she is without the drink. To make her stop almost seems a betrayal of the mother that I've always had.

I listen to my father tell stories of when she was young and they first met. She was an activist in college, a feminist, an animal rights leader. I've heard these stories before, but they stay entertaining because they remain unbelievable because my mother plans parties, cooks for her husband, and wears fur. I can only picture them if I replace the face I know with the beautiful girl from her senior photo. That girl could surely scream, run, and inspire people.

Then my father stops, and stares with a faraway look toward the mantle. He's thinking of that photo too, looking at the empty place where it used to sit. I remember when my mother took that picture down, took it down in secret, one day when my father and I were out. When we came back, it was just missing, and neither one of us bothered to ask where it went.

"You know that girl really is gone. Upstairs is just what's left of her." He sighs. "But she's mine."

"What do you mean, Dad?"

"Violet, do you think that it's possible for two people to be in love forever? To live together, and grow together. How can they be expected to go through the changes that they need to go through and come out on the other side still a good match? What are the chances of that?" He drinks. "Your mother and I, we changed, but only one of us changed in the way we were meant to. I am what I am because she deferred everything. She never made me compromise. She cost me nothing. She let the waves from my life give her a shape." He drops his voice down low, like he hopes I won't hear. "I don't love her anymore. But I made her."

I look up through the ceiling to where my mother is sleeping or drinking. In my head I see my father's story, see her beginning to drink more and speak less, drowning out that pretty girl with big dreams, all for my father, who realized too late what was happening. They're locked together now, cemented by me, my mother's lack of options and my father's guilt, and whatever measure of pain my mother can cause my father she will feel he deserves. Because all her sacrifices, made for love, to preserve love, have failed, and she has been cheated of a lifetime of changes—for nothing.

"Dad," I say as gently as I can, "when you knew, why didn't you just divorce her?"

He looks up at me, shocked. “Divorce her? You know, that’s half the problem with you kids, Violet, you think everything’s so easy. If it doesn’t fit, divorce it. If you wear it out, throw it away. I paid thirty grand for your school this year and you danced around on it barefoot.” I stand up, kiss him on the cheek again and tell him to go to bed, which is where I’m going myself. The conversation has taken a turn that I can’t stick around for. And maybe I’m proving his point, right there.

“Declare a major before the summer is over,” he says. “If you don’t, you’re not going back to school.” That stops me at the foot of the stairs. Not the threat exactly, but the option. Not going back. I never would have thought of it if he hadn’t said it, but there it is. I don’t have to go back. The world flashes clear for one brilliant second as I consider not going back. Then it’s gone, because it is, after all, just one more choice to be made. I look back at my father, still sitting on the sofa. He’s waiting for an argument.

“You know, Dad, I wasn’t suggesting that you divorce Mom.”

He says, “I know, honey,” and his face constricts. I turn to keep from seeing more. That face is the reason that he never divorced her, and why he can’t divorce her now. That face that says even though that beautiful girl is almost all gone, the boy who used to love her is still here.

◆◆◆

Waiting for Terran at a little Italian restaurant, my feet tap and twitch underneath the dark green tablecloth. I invited her out for lunch this morning and when she accepted, I felt dizzy with relief. We had exchanged so few words lately that it was like we’d been fighting. My offer of Italian, our shared favorite food, was my veiled apology.

She’s walking up; I wave to her through the window and she smiles through her sunglasses, black Prada bag slung over her shoulder. We order fast, always pasta, she’s too fit and energetic to ever sign on for this silly Atkins business. The waitress nods too approvingly at our choice, like suddenly we've become rebels, just for eating noodles.

"So you'll never guess who called me." I'm going to turn Brian into something to talk about. Something juicy, to make me new.

"Who?"

"Brian."

"Brian from school Brian?"

Even though I'm fairly sure he's the only Brian we know, I nod. "We're going out on Saturday." She asks if it's a date. I fight to keep from shrugging and say instead, "I don't know. He says he's coming through town to visit a friend. From the way it sounds, he's still with Katie."

She makes a face and tears at a breadstick, then hands half of it to me. "You could have him back, you know."

"Isn't that against your code of not stabbing girls in the back?"

"He was yours first."

"Your code has really flexible rules."

She laughs. I feel like there's so much to tell her and I'm an idiot for starting on this subject of least importance. I want to talk about Brandon. I want to tell her about my father. And I guess I want to know about Joey too because for how little I'm seeing her now, I'm seeing him even less.

But the waitress returns with the salad, and the wave of openness passes. I should keep Brandon to myself anyway, and she wouldn't understand about my father and why it matters that he doesn't love my mother anymore. Her own mother told her that she lost her heart to a boy a long time ago and didn't regret its absence. I think Terran was 8 at the time, and when 8-year-old Terran asked if that boy was her father, Meredith only laughed. Every day I am proud of her for not being a serial killer.

She coaches me through the salad on what to wear, what to say, but she's coached me before, ever since my first boyfriend.

By now I should be her protégé, but although she is the queen of charm, it is her gift only, and cannot be expanded into a commodity for other people. She's like Martha Stewart. Her absence would topple an empire if she died.

"My father's making me pick a major."

She looks up at me, startled. I had interrupted her in the middle of comparing me to Katie.

"What?"

"My father. He's making me pick a major before I go back to school."

"Or what?"

"Or he's not letting me go back at all."

"You already got in, Violet, he can't just not let you go back. You could go yourself, just get some student loans. Besides, he's probably only bluffing."

The waitress sets plates of linguine and hot marinara sauce in front of us, and Terran looks very ballsy in her white linen blouse. I watch her spin noodles around on her spoon, daring sauce to fly off in her direction.

"You know," she says, "I wasn't going to say anything, but your father has a point. If you want to graduate on time, you have to pick something now. You're already behind; you'll have to cram all of your requirements into six semesters. You've left yourself no time for more screw-off classes." I stare into my plate and think wistfully of bowling. Seeing my discontent, she sighs. "Just look through the program catalog and find something you like. You've got until August; you can declare when we get back. But the sooner the better."

She thinks I'm being lazy, but the truth is I would have chosen yesterday if I could have. She's politely telling me to hurry up, because in her eyes, the eyes of an over-achiever, my lagging behind makes me less. Not only less ambitious and less capable, but just less.

The last thing I need is someone else telling me to hurry up. The hurry is the whole problem. It's time that gives weight to our decisions, choosing a career would be nothing if we had time to infinitely change our minds. But we have only one or two chances; there is not enough life to try everything we would want to try, so we weigh our love of slam poetry against our want of a BMW; we have to be careful, practical, logical, at an age when we're entirely unfit for care, practicality, and logic.

Actually it seems stupid, making a decision that will last 40 years after only having lived 18. It seems egotistical to even try.

The weight of the decision is compounded by the fact that my career will define who I am: Am I a good doctor? A noble social worker? An unethical accountant? Maybe a lowly bank teller. Someone asks, 'What do you do?' And you reply, 'I'm a Tax Processor. I'm a paralegal. I'm a crossing guard.' I am, I am, I am. Everyone in America has become the job—who you are and what you do are no longer separate.

I look at Terran's lovely face and wish that I had an asset like that, or some great talent: singing, theorizing, discus-throwing, something that compelled me to move and left me with no choice at all as to the direction.

"Do you want to come shopping with me after lunch?" she asks. "I want to pick something up for Joey." When I ask her what, she just shrugs. She doesn't know what. Just a little something. Just a little gift. It's uncharacteristic of her. I've never known her to dote on a boyfriend. She's certainly never doted on Joey. But their relationship has changed. It has quadrupled in importance, been cracked open and stirred into something sublimely sweet and bright.

She is not behaving like herself. She is not really herself at all. Terran is gone, stuffed into a closet somewhere by Terran-In-Love. I listen to the pretty things issuing from her lips, pretty promises that Joey has made, pretty things that Joey has done, and I know that Joey is not Joey anymore either.

You can only really be yourself if you're not in love. Because love means bending, means becoming one out of two. It requires proving, and sacrifice. It distracts you from every annoyance, like a Novocaine shot against the world. You smile constantly. You start thinking in ideals. You believe that someone else's happiness and well-being are infinitely more important than your own.

In short, you behave like an absolute dodo.

Maybe I can only say this because I've never been a dodo. I've never felt that elation, except for a few vicarious, fleeting moments when Jane talked about Mr. Rochester or during the final frames of that horrible Bridges of some County movie that my mother likes so much. But if I'm right, then it's the cruelest trick ever played by the universe—that the thing that everyone searches for only robs them of themselves when they find it.

Terran is still talking and smiling about Joey. Of course, she can't tell me intimate details, to my great relief, because that would be too uncomfortable. But still, every strange word takes her farther away from where we've been. Every description becomes more difficult to imagine, until the starring roles in my head are played by faceless figures in unfamiliar clothes.

Just one meal ago she was still here with me. In the future I will look at her very carefully before speaking to ascertain just who it is that I am talking to.

Chapter 8

My parents are on their way out when Brian arrives to pick me up. They are both dressed to the nines, on their way to meet some of the partners downtown. They have only a few minutes to spare for Brian and me before they wave from the driveway. My mother looks lovely, painted and posed, nowhere near her age. She looks almost like her senior photo, if it were viewed on a TV set with bad reception.

My father gives me a nod before he ducks into the driver's seat. He hasn't mentioned our talk by the fire, but I know that he remembers. And Terran is wrong. My father doesn't bluff.

"Your dad's really important," Brian says as we walk down to his car, a sleek black Saab. I smile.

My mother once told me that the easiest way to charm a man is to get him talking about himself. That's true, although not just of men, but of everyone. I used that trick on Brian all through dinner, and now we're walking through the park, which is lit like day, and it's still working. I'm learning things about him that I never knew before. For instance, that once he happens upon the topic of himself, he's rather difficult to shut up. He's talking to me about things that he's learned at Arthur Andersen, or at school, things that make him feel intelligent for being able to speak about them: the relative efficiency of the stock market, problems with valuation models and financial reporting. He has an affection for Warren Buffett that is borderline creepy.

All of these things would be endearing, and interesting, if I loved him. They would be treasures to store in my head, remembered easily, without studying, so that I could call them up at will, proving how well I listen. Proving how well I know him. I look at him under the streetlights. He has golden hair and the brightest green eyes. I met him at a frat party and he smiled at me. I shared his bed for four months.

"Violet?"

"Yeah?"

"I miss you."

For a split second I feel real joy; he's choosing me over Katie. I'm the desirable one. I let him kiss me; I put my arms around him. For a minute I'm sucked into the game, where I have been placed in unintentional competition with my former friend. I'm desperate to take him back. Desperate to make him beg. Because by sleeping with her he has told me that I wasn't good enough, that I couldn't hold him, and that's the message that men have always sent with their promiscuity. But that's not the message we should be getting.

I push him back gently and sit down on a bench. He asks me if I think when we get back to school I might give him another chance. I tell him that I don't know. Maybe. The maybe is enough to cheer him up, and he starts talking again, picks me up off of the bench and steers me around the park. What on earth could he miss about me? We shared a bed, but not much else, and when we were together, we were usually drunk, or at least stoned. Sometimes both.

He holds my hand. I watch him talk and push the mute button in my mind. People like Brian are like models or mannequins. They remind us that we're all a little too ugly and a little too stupid. They keep us hungry and only feed us on the self-reproach that comes from being in the middle.

Yet he misses me and I barely remember him. I feel like the world has flipped its axis. If I took him back, he might make me hungry enough to wake up, tie my hair in a ponytail and chase the corporate carrot like a good girl. But even if I won there'd only be another race tomorrow, with no prize but weariness and the pats of those who have been furthered by my legs.

It's getting late and we just walk. He doesn't try to kiss me anymore or make any more plans. I keep my ears on mute and try not to put myself up on the scales with him, where he will weigh down and I will be left up high, with my legs dangling in the open air.

Two days later I scroll down the menu of my cell phone and call Katie. She answers with apprehension and I say hi.

"Oh, hi, Violet. Um, how's your summer going?"

"It's fine. Listen, Katie, I have to tell you something."

"What?"

"Do you know where Brian was this weekend?"

"Visiting his friend Kevin. Why?"

"Did he tell you that he was coming to see me too?"

"He came to see you? What for?"

"To tell me that he misses me. To ask me if I wanted to get back together."

"And do you?"

"That's not what you should be asking." I wait for her to say the right thing.

When she doesn't, I lose my patience and say, "He kissed me. And he didn't say a word about you." There is silence on the other end of the line. Maybe she'd take it better if I told her I'm not interested in him. Maybe that would put us back on the same side, even make us friends again. But I want her to figure it out on her own. That he is the one who should be shunned. I want her to strut around with Terran's girl code printed up on a T-shirt. I want us to vandalize his Saab together.

"Fuck you," she says simply, and hangs up.

I really couldn't have expected it to go any better.

◆◆◆

"Violet, stop sign!"

I slam on the brakes of Terran's Mercedes, already halfway into the intersection. Glancing in the rearview I see her and Joey wearing surprised faces, brought up closer to me by the sudden jolt. I mumble a sorry and hit the gas, a little too hard, just to get them back into their seats.

"Maybe I should drive," Joey says. There's whispering, and jostling, and I determinedly avoid looking into any of the mirrors.

"What were you daydreaming about?" Brandon asks.

"Being a foot soldier," I say, and he grins and turns to look out the window. I can't tell whether or not he thinks I was joking. But for the past 5 or 10 miles my mind has been so full of epic battles and insane bravery that I can't remember driving the distance, even though there were plenty of streetlights. I can't remember if I stopped at any of them.

And I'm still thinking about Katie and Brian. I'm pissed off that she's going to be with him, that she's going to let herself be second best. She'll probably say nothing to him about the phone call and reason it away by thinking of me as a jealous liar. Her 'fuck you' resonates back and forth between my ears, cold as ice, and that pisses me off too. She's got the nerve to think of me as the traitor, when she's the one who stole him first, and when he's the fucking lothario.

But I probably shouldn't feel like that. After all, she's the idiot who is being betrayed. Dear Abby etiquette states that you mustn't hate the victim. As penance, when I was getting ready today I dressed myself in a red shirt that is way too flashy for me and looks ridiculous. And now I'm driving to this party at Logan Allen's, when all I really want to do is sit somewhere dark and think about the guts that it took for men and horses to run screaming into spears and arrows, into blood and flying bullets. We park on the street and walk, Terran and Joey out front. As we come up on the house I sigh. All of the lights are on. There are cars wedged tightly into the driveway, and beer cans strewn like dead fish across the grass. All parties are the same; the same faces rotate through each week so the need to talk is completely diminished. The same music, the same drugs. But each week we flock to one place or another and come together in the hopes that something will happen, whether wonderful or horrible—it doesn't really matter as long as it's something. Something to be talked about later, recounted and remembered, and enlarged with each telling like some perverse game of telephone. Joey's beating of that kid a month ago was probably the best thing to happen to most of the people there. By now, in some circles Joey has almost certainly reached urban legend status.

Someone opens the door, not Logan. We might not see Logan at all, though it's his party. It's not important. We go in among loud shouts of greeting over thumping music, are all quickly handed beer cans and Terran is taken by the arm by some kid with a wood-glue Mohawk and heavy metal T-shirt whom I don't know. I watch the smoke creep up from Brandon's cigarette and hit the ceiling, dissipating like ripples on a lake. It's going to be a long night.

"Hey," Joey says, bumping my shoulder. "Terran wants to know if you want anything." He motions his head toward her and her new friend. "He says he's got good mushrooms. Some coke."

"Do you know him?" He looks just like all of the others to me, dark and dank and made up of mostly bones. He's so thin that his skin must hurt and it's us that are doing that to him, feeding off him without knowing his name, pulling pills and powder out of his insides until he's empty.

"I've seen him around," Joey says. I notice that he's looking more closely at the kid so I nudge him in the shoulder fondly. He'll take care of Terran now. He's more attentive, when it used to be that he was absolutely wasted before we even got to wherever we were going, and it was up to me to bird dog her, make sure that she stayed hydrated and didn't mix anything unfriendly.

"I don't want anything," I say. Brandon doesn't either. Joey goes back to Terran. I'm pleased to note his protective hand around her waist, and the way she leans into him. They are the most important people to each other even when they're talking to someone else. For the moment my jealousy is gone. I am fixated on them, and I hear my own shameful, secret wish: Be soul mates. Be cute, and quaint, and romantic. Be happy forever. Prove us wrong.

◆◆◆

Brandon and I were in no mood to trip, so when Terran's mushrooms kicked in we left her and Joey sitting in a semicircle with 12 other people, all passing around a bong that had lost its importance. Brandon loaded me down with beer and potato chips and we headed upstairs. I felt like I'd fallen into an old Molly Ringwald movie.

"Might as well drink slow," I caution. "They won't want to leave until they've come down, and that'll be what, 5 or 6 hours?"

"All the more reason to drink fast." He cracks open a can and hands it to me. "So what's on your mind?"

"Too much," I say and sit down next to him on the bed.

"I don't get why people say that. Like it's a virtue to be walking around with an empty head. Like they forget that it isn't feelings but thoughts that make up a soul." He grins at me. "But that's what you want, isn't it? Clarity? A skull full of nothing but water."

I have an overwhelming urge to over-dramatize any one of my issues, to make them worthy of thought in his eyes. It may be impossible. Trouble carries different weight with everyone. The death of the family dog might be just as traumatic to one person as the death of a child is to another, but the person who loses the child can never conceive that the death of the dog could carry the same weight as their own loss. Each person's trouble is his or hers alone, but I have to say something, and looking at Brandon reclined on one elbow in his now-familiar black shirt, brown hair falling into his eyes, I'm definitely not going to talk about Brian.

"My father is making me pick a major." Despite my earlier assertion to over-dramatize, my tone is flippant, betraying me, because as I've thought about it, there's a certain comfort in making the choice. The frustration and anxiety would be over. The resentment and depression could begin.

"Why are you smiling? I thought you were upset about this," he says. I force the corners of my mouth down.

I tell him that I am, and recount my feelings regarding the ridiculousness of the choice at this stage in life. He just shrugs. He says that he chose a major when he was a sophomore in high school. I mention that he can't get a job with that major and that he's twenty three and drives a Chevy that looks like a urinating beagle.

But Brandon is not unhappy. He seems completely outside of everything: outside of obligations, of fear, and maybe of practicality. There is nowhere in the world to run anymore. There is no escape from incoming streams of knowledge and needs, electricity and wires and cables and sound have bound it up tight together, one united, pulsing ball, but somehow Brandon has managed to duck the strings.

"What are you worried for," he's saying to me. "Your parents are rich and you're their only child. Tell your dad to screw off and go backpacking through Europe, as long as you have no issues with integrity."

I drink my beer in quiet. It's true. I don't have to go back at all. My parents are rich, or at least relatively so. I could essentially live off of their money forever, doing what I choose, doing nothing if I choose, if I could shake the idea that I didn't earn it. That I didn't deserve it because it didn't come from me. But I can't. That idea of worthiness is too firmly rooted in my brain and connected by a string to the eyes of other people.

I wish for a wind to blow across my surface and bring in some kind of a dream, some kind of a vision, something real. Me in a lab coat maybe, or me behind a computer screen buried up to my neck in papers. Something to want that's actually attainable, not like these silly daydreams. But even as I think that, I know that I'll never give them up, my daydreams, that like some stupid kid I can make the world magic in my head even though when I open my eyes there's only blood and dirt and concrete.

But someone will have to yank my head down and into a book sooner or later, because after all, even daydreams need funding.

Brandon cracks open two more cans and tears into the potato chips. "You know those moments of clarity you're always talking about," he pauses to chew. He looks thoughtful.

"What about them?"

He sighs, gets up and stretches, and goes to look out the window. "They're here and gone. No substance but memory." He looks at me. "They're just a feeling. Maybe a good one, but they aren't real, they can't be relived; even if you duplicate your thoughts, that clearness doesn't come back. They're just a brain anomaly, a trick. Like déjà vu."

He's telling me that I've been wasting my time—that I'm a girl waiting for a bus in the middle of a cornfield. I wonder how long he's been thinking like this and letting me ramble on like a fool. The thought makes me stubborn.

"Moments like that can keep a person sane," I say. "Moments like that are a relief."

"Moments like that only keep you searching. It's a real trick to find a life in one instant."

"But it can be done." And suddenly I know I have to believe this. I have to stretch my belief beyond the logical counterpoint, because I know that my search for clarity is really nothing more than a search for one perfect, beautiful thing. One thing with no questions.

Standing at the window, Brandon is smiling wide. "That's what I love about you, Violet. You're a cynic and a dreamer. You're a crowd of ten people who've fought to a standstill."

Love. He just said love. And he uses the word easily, not like most boys, who say it infrequently and with purpose, like a trail of sweets left on the forest floor. It occurs to me that we talk like two people on one long date. This is the talk of intriguing and of being intrigued, that lovely and foolish talk of seeing if you can be what they want, and if they can be what you want. These conversations are pulling a red veil over my eyes. I think I can hear Violet-In-Love creeping up behind me, ready to leap onto my back and choke me until I black out. Maybe I'll be quick enough to put an elbow into her eye. After all, the bitch is really out of practice.

When he holds a hand out to me I fall into his arms. His fingers slip up under my shirt, warm on my skin, then curl into the waistband of my jeans.

"You really shouldn't wear this color," he says. I know that, that's the reason that I chose it, crimson and flimsy, completely unsuited to me. It robs me of all my color, like it was my blood that was used to dye the shirt.

We kiss and there are no thrusting tongues—no saliva trail—only lips moving slowly like divers in the ocean. My heart is pounding and that is almost more interesting to me than the kiss itself. Almost.

In the next moment I hear Terran start to scream, and we break, and run through the house. There's nothing in my head except that sound, like blood in the nose of a dog. My eyes close. Open. Close. Open again, each blink like a quick flashbulb to my brain, but I can't believe what I'm seeing. I can't believe what I'm hearing, only it seems that I've gone temporarily deaf; Terran's mouth is wide open, she's clearly screaming, so why can't I hear her, why can't I hear anyone of the ten to fifteen people who have squeezed inside and are talking at her with their hands out?

She isn't stopping. She doesn't recognize them, which is not surprising she's stoned out of her mind and because their faces are all blank, slack with shock, washed completely free of their normal expressions.

Something has to be done. She's starting to claw at herself, and the bed sheet has fallen away from her body. I can see her underwear lying in a crumple on the floor. The scene makes no sense. I've stopped blinking in an effort to slow things down. Joey is by the bed, his shirt off, his pants unbuttoned. I hear him say, "Violet, she just flipped," and his arms flutter uselessly toward her. I finally move closer to pull the sheet back up and to bind her arms. Joey keeps on explaining, he says things that I'll only really think about later, that it was supposed to be their first time; that everything was ruined, that he's sorry, so sorry, really incoherent dribble shit like that. My brain lets his words float through. The only message I get is that he shouldn't be saying that here, because even if this crowd of people have no faces they still have ears. I look at Terran. Her pupils are so dilated that her blue eyes have gone black and alien. The screaming stops and she says my name. I can hear Brandon ordering people out of the room, shoving them if they won't leave the ring. When they're gone he shuts the door, soft but firm and stands in front of it.

I get her dressed and calm her down. Joey brings water from the adjacent bathroom. I get her to sip, big eyes over the cup watching me. She's like a beautiful child.

"We should get her out of here," Brandon says. I nod and pull her up; she's so high that she's collapsible. Picking her up is like handling an oversized marionette. She's risen still clutching the sheet so I wrap her tighter in it. Out of the corner of my eye I see Joey reach down and pick up Terran's panties. He doesn't look up as he shoves them in his pocket.

When we come out of the room and head down the stairs the whispers stop, the silence spreading before us like a red royal carpet. Terran is wrapped up in the white sheet and I have my arms around her. I flash my eyes angrily at all of the eyes upon us. I can see it on all of their faces: excitement and curiosity masked with concern. I try to wrap her up tighter in the sheet, and beside us Joey is still mumbling his inept apologies.

"Shut up!" I shout at all of them, but shouting in vain, because dozens of recording eyes are on this scene, and in their minds they've already given it a headline. The Night that Terran Ingram was raped at Logan Allen's Party.

When we get out onto the front steps I hear someone call my name. I turn to see Logan, making his appearance at last. He glances at Terran with a sour look, and then says to me, "Keep her quiet about this, huh Violet? My parents would kill me." Then he shuts the door.

Chapter 9

"I don't know where to go," Brandon says from the driver's seat. Joey is beside him in the passenger seat, not daring to look back. I'd like to tell him to drive to Joey's house, open the door and kick him out rolling. But then Brandon would go too, and the twitch of Terran's shoulders beneath the sheet tells me that I can't handle her by myself yet.

"The gorge," I say and he turns left. It's familiar and still and pretty. It might be enough to pull her out of the hole that the mushrooms have made her crawl into. I hope so. Because she's still got at least four hours of tripping left, and a whole world of shit could rain down between now and then.

When we get there I'm thankful for the full moon, the perfect silver nightlight, except I hope that the shimmers on the leaves don't make her trip harder. Joey is leaning into the backseat, trying to touch her. It's making her cringe. She frowns and her head rolls back against me like a rag doll's.

"Get out," I say to him when the car stops. I leave Terran curled up quietly on the backseat and quickly tuck her blonde hair behind her ear. "Can you stay with her?" I ask Brandon.

"Yeah. But if she wants you, I'm going to bring her to you."

I nod and stalk off toward the rocks, the moonlight letting me walk as fast as I like and Joey had better be right behind me. When we get to the boulders I spin hard, right in his face. "What is the matter with you?"

He starts in with his explanations, she wanted to, she flipped out, he'd never hurt her, he's sorry but it wasn't his fault. Every new word comes out of his mouth so easy, and they make me want to scream until my vocal cords fly out of my throat.

"She's on hallucinogenic drugs, Joey."

"So what? She's always been fine before. You've been there, you've never seen her flip."

"You're not."

"I'm not what?"

"You're not ON anything!" I shout and the night around us makes the volume of my voice indecent, but I don't care. He's not on anything, he's stone cold sober and he's not an idiot. He knew what he was doing. "You raped her."

He tells me to shut up. I blink at him. My friend Joey who just raped our friend Terran and now he's standing in front of me with shitty explanations and his lower lip pushed out like a petulant child. So I hit him. Once, hard, and then again. I've never hit him before, but now I'm going to slap his face off and I'm crying before he even hits me back. Which he does. I end up lying in the damp grass with my cheek hot and the wind knocked out of me, which is good because otherwise I would scream at him until my lungs bleed. He tries to help me up, but I kick at him and call him a fucker. Then I just lay there staring at the cold stars. My anger came up so fast and so intensely; I can feel it in the back of my throat, heavy and choking, a little cloud of it waiting to form into words. I can feel it in my wrists and hands, in the way that they shake. It's an itchy little tingle. I hadn't meant to hit him. I think that now, and I mean it, but a moment ago I know that I meant to kill him, if only I were stronger or had a rock in my fist. Is this what it's like for him every time? This ridiculous rage? It's a disgusting, remorseful, uncontrollable feeling, and it embarrasses me. I hadn't thought I was capable of it, but now it's here and so easy—like it has been here all along, pretending to be asleep while peering out with one secret eye. I'm no different from him. I could scream obscenities into a stranger's face. I could spin someone's neck around with a baseball bat. I think I could look into a mirror and see my eyes gone blood red, all of my veins standing out black against my white skin. I feel sickly human.

"I'm sorry," Joey spits down at me, but his voice is still pissed off and he doesn't sound like he means it. "Are you hurt?"

"Of course not." My face still stings, but it's nothing to whine about.

"That was a really shitty thing to say, Violet."

"Not really," I mutter, pushing resolutely off the ground and climbing to my feet. "But I suppose that it was a really shitty thing to hear."

"I would never hurt her," he says.

"Never doesn't exist," I spit. The heat of the moment is leaking out of me as quickly as it came, washing away with the sound of the water behind us until we're alone again with our mutual concern.

"I'm going back to her now. Stay out here by the rocks until I send Brandon over."

"You can't."

"She doesn't want you right now, Joey," I snap. It sounds so jealous, and I'm ashamed of myself again, because part of me is glad. She'll have to see now what a mistake this is, that he's still the same old Joey.

I turn my back on him and start walking.

"She'll forgive me," he says, his voice teetering between sulky and sad.

"I know," I say through clenched teeth, and he grabs my wrist.

"You'll forgive me too."

Of course I will. But I tug away and keep walking.

◆◆◆

One long night spent fixing Terran, of first stroking her hair and then following her out of the SUV, trailing her as she scampered along the grass like a monkey, full of wonder, the blood blooming in her brain and it was making everything extraordinary. She spun and laughed and cried, all the same to her. She was fixated on my shirt for twenty minutes. By the time it was over and I could get her back to the truck, Joey was back inside with Brandon. They were both asleep and the sky had gone a cornflower blue.

Now I'm awakened by her smoking, and I know that it's far too damn early. I don't know how she does that, trips hard or drinks hard and wakes up fresh. But she's beautiful again, joint pressed between her lips and when she sees my eyes crack open she leans forward and exhales into my face, smoke blasting against my pillow like fog in a hard rock video. I give her the finger and she laughs, a little sad though and then she says,

"Thank you for last night, Violet."

I shrug gently. "Are you okay?"

She looks away, and taps her fingernails on her teeth. She doesn't have to say anything. It's plain on her face that the rape of last night is a million miles away. The entire memory of it will be kept separate from her, conveniently contained within the drugs. She's shaking her head and raising her brows, but it's not to say that no, she isn't okay. It's to say that she doesn't even think of it as rape. She's not upset. She's just embarrassed. She feels stupid, but it hasn't done any lasting damage. And she certainly doesn't blame Joey. Of course she doesn't. Let's not forget that she's Terran-In-Love. When she looks back at me there's a big apology in those green eyes.

"Don't," I say. "You buy the Italian and we'll call it even."

She smiles. "Deal," and slides up off of the bed.

"Where are you going?" I ask, even though I know.

"I have to see Joey."

"Today?" She's going to apologize to him. I want to shake her and slap her and tell her to slap him, but Terran-In-Love would only blink back at me stupidly.

"Yeah. Tomorrow I'm at work all day and then I have dinner with my mother and my grandparents." She checks herself in the mirror, spotless. I ask her softly what ever happened with her B-plus, and she shrugs. For all its drama, Joey has made it much less important. She's standing bravely beneath her mother's threats and insults, a dream of Joey as a parasol above her head.

What has happened to her own brand of clarity that she possessed only a few weeks ago? What has stopped her thinking that she is only one of many; that no one is special, that relative happiness can be found with an almost infinite number of people? What has white-washed her mind, erasing all of those broad strokes?

It seems impossible that it could be only Joey. But I have no doubt that it is.

◆◆◆

My mother and I walk into the house with brown paper sacks in our arms, each filled with produce from the farmer's market. It was a long morning of strolling and squeezing and weighing things in our hands. My mother smiled at me behind her big Jackie-O sunglasses even though it wasn't bright out, sunglasses to hide the red veins in her eyes from too much wine or gin the night before. I said nothing, only smiled back. I'm worse than my father, no longer loving her and screaming at her flaws, because I do love her I remain silent while she marches on toward an inevitable case of cirrhosis. I value her tremulous smile more than her life.

Everything we purchased gets placed into large bowls, mostly for display. She bought yellow peppers just for looks. We all hate them. And there they sit in the center of the kitchen counter, towers of shining reds and yellows and greens, setting off the orange of the tulips on the table. I inhale deeply. My mother's house is filled with flowers and yet it has no smell. She is meticulous and disciplined, and standing here in her kitchen we're like a pair of mismatched shoes.

When I was young she used to tell me that I was an odd child, but she said it with such affection, with such quiet eyes, that I used to think it was a compliment. And maybe it was. Maybe she saw my oddness as a virtue back then; perhaps she thought I'd grow up to be something special and original, some kind of an artist. How disappointed she must be.

When my father comes in from an early nine holes of golf, she turns away and looks busy cleaning. He kisses me on the cheek and asks if I want a sandwich.

"Have you made any decisions yet?" He's leaning into the refrigerator when he asks this and the question seems to come out of his ass. I have an overwhelming urge to laugh, or to say, 'about what,' but if I want that sandwich, I'd better not.

"Not yet. But I've been thinking about it." Which is, at least, true. He comes out of the fridge, his arms laden with mustard and mayo, deli-sliced chicken. Without missing a beat, my mother dives in behind him, going after the cheese and lettuce.

"It can't be that difficult, Violet," he scolds, getting out bread and slapping it with mustard. "I decided when I was a freshman in high school to go into finance like my father, and your mother decided young to focus on literature and poetry because she was passionate about the arts." I notice that he didn't add a justification on the end of his degree like he did to hers, maybe to point out that her degree was pointless and I'd be unwise to choose it. "You just have to identify your strengths."

I instantly think of my 135 bowling average. I bite my tongue on that and wait until I have my sandwich to say, "Dad, I'm not good at anything. But I'm okay at everything. I'm a walking, talking B-minus. Which on the upside, means that I could do just about anything. Of course, it also means that no matter what I choose, I'm not going to be that great at it."

He tells me that I won't get anywhere with that attitude, or something else clichéd like that. Something pops into my head, and I spout off some rhetoric that one of my professors said during his introductory speech, that mine is the first generation that isn't expected to do better than the generation before it. Forty pens skidded to a stop in the classroom that day, as that professor smiled up at us from his pulpit at the better part of history. Welcome to the Dawn of the Death of Optimism 101.

"Just because I've done well doesn't give you the right to slack off. It is still possible to do better, or at least to do just as well. How do you think I got here anyway? It wasn't by being unfocused until I was twenty. It was a lot of hard work. It's still hard work. That's what's wrong with you kids. None of you want to work. You think that you're entitled to something just for being born. You've been spoiled by Ritalin and psychotherapy, by structured snack times and padded playgrounds. None of you have ever learned to climb. Or how to get back up after you fall."

My father's eyes are very bright as he says this, because he believes it with his whole heart. It is that secret thing that he thinks when he sees all young children, all teens, and me; that we've all become too soft, and that thought lets him stand up taller, prideful of his own generation's toughness. I suddenly feel my arms linked with every kid in America, every kid who sticks out their tongue or smokes pot or writes a thesis that reads like the Communist Manifesto.

"We're not afraid of hard work. But maybe we want our rewards now. We want the time to live our lives now, while we've still got the youth to live it."

"You have no patience. It takes dedication and time," he says, interrupting me.

But I've seen him work hard, and then harder. Now he seems to be edging past his prime and still working, and the cars, and the house, and all of the other expensive toys he's got are all underused. Maybe once he thought he would work until he had all that he could enjoy. Maybe he thought that someday he could look around him and stop. That he would get there. That he would make it. But ambition has him by the wrist. He's never going to get there. There's always going to be one step more, and when he stops finally he'll be old, and it will be hard, because by then he'll be working for the work, and he'll have forgotten anything that he loved besides that ambition. My father is an icon of the American Dream. I've watched him do it. I know what it takes. I know what it gets you. And I haven't been at all convinced into holding out my wrist. I finish my sandwich and kiss him on the cheek. This is yet another thing that we can't understand about each other. Understanding between us is a dream made of sugar. It happens to everyone, this unsympathetic, generational gap. As I leave the kitchen I hear my mother following me, all the way up the stairs, but she doesn't stop me until I'm at my bedroom door.

"I know what your father told you," she says, and for a moment I'm mortified, thinking she knows that he doesn't love her. "That he won't pay for school unless you declare a major before the end of the summer." I nod mutely. She glances over her shoulder, back toward the stairs so I open the way to my bedroom and we step inside. It's been ages since we've been in here together and it feels somehow too small for us, but after a few moments we sit down on the bed, my mother sitting and rearranging and sitting again, like a very pretty cat with wet feet.

"He'll pay for it," she says bluntly.

"I still don't know what I want to do."

"He'll pay for it anyway."

"You think he's bluffing?"

"No. But if he doesn't pay for it, I'll leave him and pay for it myself out of the divorce settlement." I feel as though I've stuck my finger into an outlet. The casual way that my mother has just said that she could divorce my father, and use me as an excuse to do it has sent a jolt through me. And she's sitting there in her smart linen shirt, presenting herself to me as a very surprising ally.

"Why would you do that?" I don't believe her. I don't think she'd go through with it. I want to know the real reasons why she's saying this, because I know that it isn't for me, it has something to do with them. I think that I may become the project of my mother's midlife crisis.

"Because you have to go to school," she says simply.

I nod. And I feel like a shit because it is for me that she's saying it, and I think she'd actually do it too. If the goodness or badness of a person is defined not by what they say, or what they do, which can be false, but by the judgments cast in their heads, then I am basically rotten.

"I won't let your father hold you up by your puppy scruff," she says, smiling. She won't let him control me even though she can't stand up for herself. And something else that I realize as we're sitting on this bed: She thinks that I'm strong. I can see it in her admiring eyes. I don't know where she got the idea, because I really don't feel like I have any sort of will. Maybe it's because she often sees me alone. Maybe it's because she's never seen my judgment clouded by the love of a boy; she's never seen me bend. "You'll go to school," she says, daydreaming on my face. "And you'll be something great." In the end, they both want the same thing, my mother and my father—only they want it for different reasons. My father wants me to go to school and be successful so that I will be like him, to prove that his life is worthy of envy. My mother wants me to go so that I'll never be like her, to prove that her life was a price that she didn't have to pay.

◆◆◆

I'm in the elevator of Terran's mother's building, going up to see if Terran can go out for lunch. I want to tell her about my mother; I want to tell her about kissing Brandon. I just want to talk to her, maybe about none of those things, maybe just about garlic bread. I'm excited to see her; after the other night when she needed me so badly I feel like our friendship has been re-cemented. When a bike messenger gets into the elevator with me, I smile and press his button for him, thankful that it's only June and not August so he doesn't smell completely rank.

We step out together and he heads off to the receptionist's area. I stand and look down one way and then the other, the whole place done in white and silver, glass doors, high ceilings, very minimalist and scientific. I don't wait long before I see her, in a black suit, striding through the room 20 feet in front of me. But before I can open my mouth to call out, or raise a hand to wave, someone runs up behind her, handing her papers, and two others come up after that, and she's talking to them very fast, and each one bobs their head in turn like seagulls at the park waiting to be thrown a bread crust.

There is an energy in this place that runs so thick that I think my hair must be standing up because of it. There are so many people nodding and pointing, at her and because of her. It doesn't look like any internship I've ever heard of. The girl in front of me in the crisp black suit and stark blue shirt is no glorified copy-girl. She's not getting coffee or taking meeting notes. She's running the meetings. She's Meredith Ingram Jr., and she looks like she belongs here, like college is just a formality. I feel stupid, showing up unannounced and trying to pull her away from all of this. I'm a silly, plain girl standing in the middle of the reception area with a bag slung over my shoulder. And when Terran finally sees me, pausing amid all of the chatter to gaze at me, unblinking, there's something so dead and wolverine in her eyes that I turn around and leave the way I came. When I get into the elevator, I push the button to shut the doors quickly and don't look out to see whether she is still staring.

Chapter 10

Something is tapping on my window. Tapping me out of a very nice daydream, a daydream set against a backdrop straight out of Wuthering Heights. I was almost asleep, and I think for a moment in my grogginess that it's only a twig, except there's no tree by my window. Maybe it's a bird. An angry bird, or a bat maybe, and if it is, I'm just going to let it in here because I'm tired and I really don't give a flying fig.

I reach my hand out to pull back the curtain and a rain of pebbles strikes the glass. If this is Joey, I'm going to drop my stereo onto his head. I wait a few seconds, but there isn't another volley so I get up and open the window, then stick my head out. It's muggy; central air goes rushing out around me to die just past my shoulders.

Down on the lawn is Brandon, waving with a big stupid grin on his face. I almost ask him what he wants, but that's a very stupid question.

"Hang on," I say, and shut the window and go downstairs. When I get outside he puts his fingers to his lips and takes my wrist. He is headed for his car. I can smell the 80-proof cloud floating around his head so I pull in the other direction. There is a park a few blocks over, with swings to create a breeze. A late June heatwave has struck tonight, and you can sweat just standing, even in the dark.

"How did you know which window was mine?"

"I guessed." Brandon grins.

"What if you had guessed wrong and gotten my parents?"

He shrugs. "I don't know. Maybe ran. Maybe asked for directions to your window." He laughs. "I really don't know. I'm pretty drunk." He is—he's wavering on his feet. I wonder where he's been. He says that he just wanted to see me. I'm touched; I suppose I've been touched since the moment I stuck my head out and saw him standing on my lawn like a '50s fairy tale. If I had a trellis, I bet he would have climbed it.

We get to the park, find the swings, and sway back and forth, but after a few minutes he stops and gets up. Then he just kind of collapses in the grass. He has got his eyes closed.

"I thought you wanted to see me."

"Still do," he replies. "But I suspect that the park is spinning."

I sit down next to him and stroke his hair. I don't know what it is about him that makes him more interesting than the other boys in the world, but I do know it's probably a quality that's present only in my own head. I'm probably just inventing some great interest because I'm attracted to him. By making him special I'm justifying an irrational feeling. Am I becoming Violet-In-Love? I don't know. I look at his mouth and remember kissing it, and there is a definite pull, a very acute temptation. But I refuse it. No pretty boy is going to turn me into an idiot.

Those lips move as I watch them; he tells me to talk about something, to keep him awake. That's a good idea because if he passes out here in the park, I'm going to have to just leave him.

After a few minutes of me not thinking of anything, he asks if my father is still pressuring me into a decision. I stretch out on the grass and say yes, and give him the update, about my mother, about my father's view of our respective generations. It still seems stupid to me, this hundred thousand dollar decision, though it must matter, it must be extremely important, because it wouldn't cost so much if it didn't. I know my father wants me to choose finance, and it'd be almost easy to just pick that to please him, except that I'd have to see his shaking head for the rest of my life as he came to terms with the fact that I am only a mediocre financier. Having me fail at his success would prove me the ultimate failure of his loins.

I know my mother wants me to choose something impassioned and independent, something like a lawyer maybe, where I will walk everywhere with a briefcase and a power suit, with the song 'Sisters Are Doing It for Themselves' constantly playing in the background. But I can't see spending fourty years that way, either way, working and working, transforming from person into job, pursuing tiny little bits of happiness in my scant spare time. Sometimes the image of the future is too big, too abstract and intimidating. And the future goes on to forever. "Tell me that life is short and I'll give you the finger," I finish.

Brandon says, "Life is short. Short when it's good and long when it's bad. The measure of time changes within our heads, and only there. When it's short, you stress for more, you mourn its passing, you try to bask in it, stretch it out for one long, relaxing moment. And when it's long you try to fill it up, whip it into a run, waiting for that next second when you'll want to rein it in."

Of course we've all felt the things he's saying. Time is a silver eel sliding around our bodies, at once beautiful and a nuisance. There's never really too much or too little of it. There's just time, beyond bottling or manipulating by the human brain, never mind that we rush and push and use ridiculous phrases like "saving it" or "buying it." Brandon and I are young, and for us even a span of thirty years is difficult to imagine. There's so much still to pass, laughably insignificant things that will fade to a dot and disappear on the line of this incomprehensible thing that doesn't end.

I get up and drag Brandon up off the ground to take him up to my room so he can sleep it off on my floor.

"I am really glad that we have these talks, Violet," Brandon whispers sheepishly. I only nod. I realize suddenly that we will never do this again. As we stumble back to my house the knowledge of this makes me sad.

◆◆◆

In the kitchen the next morning there was bacon, eggs, and an odd sort of tension. My father was in the paper, as usual, my mother cooking, as usual, but they treated me with a delicate sort of care, the kind of care that says that they'd like to ask a question, maybe several, but they just can't quite decide how to do it.

It has mostly to do with the fact that Brandon spent the night; he came downstairs with me and burst into the kitchen. I don't know why they were surprised, his car was still parked in the driveway, but they were both horrified—smiling and horrified as he praised my mother's eggs. Brandon took it all in stride. He made small talk with my father and joked with my mother. Then he kissed me on the cheek, thanked them for their hospitality, and took his leave.

If they'd only ask, they could know that nothing really happened; that I just brought him home and put him to bed and played good hostess by sleeping on the floor. But they don't ask, so I just sit and wait for my French toast, paging through one of my mother's Martha Stewart Living magazines, which is full of silly elegance and inventive ways to make napkin holders out of tree bark. I pause to watch my mother arrange lilies in a tall crystal vase and ask, "Mom, where will you get your ideas for toilet paper origami if Martha Stewart goes to prison?" She tells me not to be smart, that she has never once folded the toilet paper. My father tells me that if Martha the person goes to prison, Martha Stewart the company will carry on. He says that a company might start with one person, but it doesn't end with one. I look down at the two-page spread resting on the table, the blonde sophisticate smiling in the midst of red photographs, glorifying five different uses for boysenberries, and think that he might be wrong.

My mother goes to answer a knock at the door, and to my surprise, comes back with Joey. He's standing in the kitchen archway, one hand in his pocket, the other out to shake my father's hand, all the while looking at me with his lopsided smile. My mother asks him if he has eaten breakfast, and he says yes, but comes over to my plate and takes a bite of my toast anyway.

"Want to go for a drive?" he asks.

◆◆◆

Frankly I don't know why I said yes. Joey's driving has always made my stomach climb up and down my spine, and today is no different. We're out on quiet highway 23, doing eighty five on a road that is far too curved for eighty five. But after 10 miles of this he slows down and stops, turns around, and drives us to the gorge, we don't get out and go to the rocks. We just sit in the car with the A/C blasting.

"I haven't seen you in a while," he says.

"Well, I've been around." I respond. It isn't fair to pass the blame onto him. I could've called too. Then again, he raped our mutual best friend, so I suppose the ball was really in his court. Reading my mind, he asks if I'm still mad. I shake my head. After all, if Terran's not mad, then what right do I have to be?

"Terran says she's sorry about the other day when you saw her at the office. She wants to get together and have lunch or something."

I am really unaccustomed to him knowing everything first the old bitterness is at the back of my throat again. "What, did her cell phone break?"

He blushes. He actually blushes, I wonder about the meaning behind that blush, the meaning behind it when he says a little grudgingly that they've been spending a lot of time together, that they're almost inseparable.

"You were always inseparable," I say.

"No," he says. "*We* were always inseparable. All of us. The three of us." He lights up a cigarette, looks so cool, a real new millennium James Dean or something. I watch his profile. He's not looking at me when he's talking, and that makes me think he means it, that the touchy feely stuff is making him uneasy. But I can't believe it, not really, when he's always been in love with her and her alone, when all of the time spent just him and me were only moments spent together waiting for her.

Except that I remember other things suddenly, like he used to wait for me sometimes to drive me home, that he used to hold a book over my head if it were raining until I pushed it away to get wet, that he cheated off of my math homework even though Terran was 10 times better at it than either of us. He made me jump off the rock cliffs and into the river. He gave me my first smoke.

So why have I always felt that our friendship has been like people in a waiting room, reading magazines and making small talk, checking our watches to see when our appointments with Terran were due? That we were together, but not to see each other. There's a big stab of guilt thinking it was all me, that it was only me thinking that way all along. But it couldn't have been. Something has brought me to the foreground of his mind, and maybe not even me, but just my presence, and that something is relatively new.

He looks kind of sad and distant, like he's not even listening to himself. He used to talk a little about suicide in high school, and it flashes through my mind that he might be thinking like that again. But if he is, I'll never know it—that kind of talk is almost reserved for high school. Melodramatic, teen angst. We're supposed to grow out of it.

I remember one of our conversations from back then. It was right after he told me that he should have died a long time ago, and he asked me about suicide. He never threatened it, never talked of it like an option. He just brought it up in a roundabout way. What did I think of it? At the time I told him that it was wrong—that you weren't given this life just to throw it away. I was a silly kid regurgitating words from an after-school special. Those words don't sound anything like me, and I want that conversation to do over again. I'd make up a better argument, or I'd answer the actual question and think of it on my own terms. Because suicide was then, and is now, just too big a commitment for me. Forget all the theological finger-shaking and the other moral shit. Suicide is death, and death is done, final, the ultimate in binding contracts. And no one really knows what lies beyond it. Puppies? Maybe. Pain? Maybe. Or maybe it's an eternal thumb war with Roseanne Barr. Either way, it's too uncertain and permanent a condition to ever enter into willingly.

He passes me a cigarette and I take it because it fits my mood. Maybe I'm over analyzing him. Maybe what I'm seeing in the driver's seat next to me is just Joey-In-Love, except I thought that that was the only Joey whoever existed.

"I want to take you up to the lake house for your birthday," he says, his smile suddenly back.

My birthday. July 5th. I'll be nineteen. Tick tock. I wonder whose idea the lake house was. As I look at his grin, I know it was his. "Terran's going too of course," I say. He looks away and nods. He says we can stay the whole week if we want to; she's got the time off. He says this the way that I'm thinking it, that it's a convenient way for her to get out of that office. We talk about her for a while and things feel back to normal, aside from the fact that

Joey's doing most of the talking and I'm mostly absorbing. He says that she hates her job, and her mother, but these are things that I already knew.

Finally I ask the thing that I've wanted to know since he brought up the birthday excursion, the thing that makes me faintly ashamed.

"Is Brandon coming?"

"Sure," he says, in a little boy voice that tells me he was hoping it would just be the three of us. But things have changed and that's no longer possible.

◆◆◆

I'm surprisingly excited about the trip to the lake. July fourth couldn't come fast enough. It's been a long time since we've been up to Joey's parents' vacation house—practically years since we've all piled into a car and driven the long highway lined with pines. Terran's moving along at her usual 80 miles per and Brandon's playing DJ, keeping our ears full of American Hi-Fi, Rusted Root, and Bad Religion.

When we get there nothing's changed. It's perfect, this golden-brown log house, and it could be my twelfth birthday rather than my nineteenth. Bags over our shoulders, we stare up at the two stories of our own history, the same three peony bushes, the same porch swing that Joey broke his nose falling off of and the lake, which is actually two lakes, connected by a channel just wide enough to boat through, just visible through the trees.

"I don't know why we don't come up here more often," Terran says, and Joey says, "Because ordinary ruins fantasy," this this makes my ears perk up. It's a very un-Joey-like thing to say. But I ignore it for the moment, and walk slowly up the front steps, preserving the nostalgia, awaiting the even larger rush of when Joey opens the doors.

When we finally walk in, I wish everyone would stop moving around so much, stop throwing down bags and checking the refrigerator, and just stand and see what I see, a place that time hasn't touched. Nothing has changed. It even still smells the same, like pine and hydrangeas, and walking into it is like jumping into a frame of our old lives. When I look down at my chest, I'm frankly surprised to have breasts.

Joey breaks the spell, lifting me into a shaking hug, growling 'happy birthday' into my ear. I grin, and look over to see Terran with a troubled look on her face that she quickly covers with a grin of her own.

"Get into your suit," he says to me. "Brandon and I'll go get the boat ready."

◆◆◆

Terran is so tense that she trembles as she changes, her tanned back to me as she fumbles with the straps of her coral pink bikini. Just when I'm about to ask her what's the matter, she gives a little choke-sob and flops down on the bed, her face in her hands.

"Here," I say and take the straps from her as she holds the top on, tie it quickly around the back of her neck and hook it tight around her ribs. She's mumbling something I can't quite understand. I move away to tie my own suit. She shuts up immediately, blocking words with the back of her hand like she might vomit them instead of just talk, so I put my hand back on her shoulder so that she can borrow my will and go on.

I listen while she tells me about her mother's psychotic expectations, details I didn't get from Joey, the extra hours, the assignments that were far too advanced, so that she had to pore through third-year textbooks over her lunch breaks. The voice that she tells me in is restrained, just one step up from tears and one step over from screaming. She's choking. Suffocating. Being squeezed into a box by her mother's eyes. I don't tell her that those are eyes that she has inherited.

"This is what my life is," she says, her voice still carrying that strong, froggy quality, like a horse with its mouth tugged back tight by the bridle. "And no one ever asked me what I wanted." She looks back at me. "Not even you."

I find that hard to believe, after all of the talking we've done, but maybe she's right. Her life has been laid out. There have been no questions of how or why, just when, and if there were ever an alternative, we simply must have missed it.

"Well, what do you want?" I ask her now.

"How should I know? When have I ever had the time to figure it out?" She laughs, and I smile, sad smile and sad laugh, and in the grand scheme of starving children and murdered grandmothers, I suppose this doesn't count for much. But suffering is suffering, and maybe hers will be worse, because it will be prolonged, and because no one will ever sympathize.

She says that she's been watching me struggle with my decision for weeks, and she envies me my choice. She envies me. It would seem ridiculous if I weren't coming to believe that discontent is the human condition.

"Look," I say. "It's just the stress you're under. And being up here. Back at the lake house, it's put us all in a weird mood. Me, for example. I'm so flipping nostalgic right now that I could pass you a note and give Joey a makeover.

"You'll shake all of this off," I say. "You'll succeed at anything, you know that. We all know that." She gets up, pulls khaki shorts on over her swimsuit and waits for me at the door. She's staring at me like I'm a traitor. I look deep, deep into her eyes and count to three, hoping to see an irrational girl. But it's only Terran.

◆◆◆

After the lake wore us out with its rocking, we made our way into the little pub on the main street of the little town, the same one we always went to when we were younger.

Usually it's full to bursting with affluent vacationers, but tonight it's relatively quiet; it's only Wednesday and most of the holiday crowd won't get in until the morning of July fourth.

Our bellies are lined with burgers and seasoned fries, and now we're topping them off with beer, beer in nice cold bottles, so much nicer than out of a can, and more dignified than out of a keg. Joey calls for another round, and then another. The heat of the day accelerates our drunk. When they shake me back to consciousness, I'm basically wasted and I have no idea how we've all gotten into Joey's dad's boat and back out into the middle of the lake in the middle of the night. There's a tequila shot under my nose, and it makes me reel. I look over the side at the inky water, think quickly of things sliding around in it, of things dying in it and decomposing and dispersing. It's creepy and unclean and I pull my head back over into the boat.

"Isn't that a little dangerous out here," I ask, nodding toward the shot glasses.

"Don't worry," Brandon says, "I've got limes and salt in my pockets." That's not what I meant of course, but it's my birthday and I take the shot, suck on a lime that was cut with a dull pocketknife so most of the juice leaked out during the carving. If anything, the taste of the shot brings me back into my brain. I can relax for a minute and watch the moon re-create itself on each ripple.

"I think we should help Violet solve her problem," Terran says suddenly. "As a birthday gift. I think we should help her decide what to do with her life." She's grinning at me. I can't tell if she's being serious or not, if she's brought this up to be helpful or hurtful. She's leaning against the captain's chair with her arm slung around Joey, who I think is staring at me, but he's all shadow so I can't be sure.

Brandon moves over to sit next to me and refill my shot glass. "Well she can't make the decision herself," she says. "She can't figure out the difference between what she wants, and what she's supposed to want."

Joey and Brandon have nothing to offer. Brandon because he's too busy listening, and Joey because he doesn't understand the weight of the decision. He never felt the weight of his own. Why would he? He's so sure that he won't be alive long enough to deal with the consequences.

"When did the American Dream become so boring?" Terran laughs softly. "Picket fences three kids, and stupid women who want to do it all: mother, wife, president, slut; you'd think we'd found a way to clone time—that we've evolved to have twice the muscle since the 1950s, when it's really only Xanax and Ephedrine. Botox and silicone." She takes another shot, violently, and wipes her mouth with the back of her hand.

"Hey," Joey says while giving her a sharp look, he kisses her, giving her a little shake.

I reach for the tequila bottle and pour Terran a quarter shot, lifting my own glass high into the air. She's upset and although we know why, there's no empathy in us. So Joey will do what he can, and I will do what I can, which is get her drunker even though Brandon says it's not a good idea—we're probably all past the "able to swim" stage should we happen to capsize. I tell him that I don't care, it's my birthday and I want that four on the floor thing, whatever that is. So I hold up my glass and say, "Here's to no longer being a draining, pathetic loser," and we drink.

◆◆◆

I was born on July fifth. The day after the celebration. When I was a little girl, adults would always 'ooh' at that, like I missed being really special by twenty four hours. I always thought it was rather polite of me, not spoiling my parents' Fourth of July picnic with my birth, and deferring the glory of the day to America instead. I was born a patriot, except now that word always comes out sounding sarcastic.

This July fourth is hot. The lake is filled to the edges with people and machines, all wearing decorations and holiday faces, and the screaming children are doing nothing for our headaches. Joey maneuvers the boat into open water and speeds up to generate a breeze. It's still not very fast; little black dragonflies skating across the surface like miniature helicopters have no trouble keeping pace, doing their best to evade attacking bass.

We spent the morning eating eggs and the afternoon nursing jelly legs and weak stomachs, until finally we were brave enough to get drunk again, and then drunk enough to get back out onto the water. Joey stops the boat, lets us drift and comes to the back to hand me an ice cold glass of rum punch. I smile, but I get up and go sit next to Brandon, leaving Joey fluttering. He eyeballs all of the empty space surrounding Terran and then trudges back to the captain's seat. He's been doting on me since we got up here, and not just because it's my birthday. It's too noticeable. This morning in the kitchen, Terran said to me quietly, "He's paying a lot of attention to you," then quickly left before I could realize whom she was talking about. At first it made me angry, but now I'm thinking of the look on his face when he said that they were inseparable, and I'm watching the open space next to her stay open.

Something between them was slipping, and far sooner than I expected. They're breaking apart, proving me right. For a minute I can't breathe; I'm so shocked by the sadness that I feel. I drink hard and long, and make the rum hurt my throat, pushing all of the other stuff down because my pity is hypocritical—I never wanted them to set hands on each other in the first place. That of course made me a bad friend, but I still can't say I was wrong because really, does anyone ever want their friends to fall in love? When all it promises is a new element of complication, and that you will be relocated to a position of less importance?

And less importance is an understatement. The old adage of 'friends before lovers' doesn't hold. Love is selfish. It has to be the most important thing, the end-all-be-all of existence. Who wrote that line, 'All you need is love'? It wasn't the Beatles. It was actually love itself.

Now love, that busy bee, has stung Terran and Joey, had pulled its own guts out trying to free itself.

I wonder when it started to happen, and how. Was it a hand brushed away or was it a forced smile? When was that little, fragile moment when one lover ceases to feel and the other comes to know it? I'll never know, not really, no matter who tells me what in the end. I'll never know who messed it up—was she too needy or was he too clingy? It was probably neither one of them, although sooner or later someone will have to be blamed. The sad truth is, it's ending because it ends, and that's that.

Brandon is watching the scene too, though with less surprise on his face. Maybe he's been more perceptive, or maybe living with Joey there's just more to perceive. No one could miss it now; the growing distance between them has taken a solid form, the air has gone chalky with confusion and unspoken things.

Brandon runs his fingers down the back of my neck, cold fingers covered with beer bottle sweat. I close my eyes.

Terran starts to talk to Brandon loudly about his plans for the future, listening intently when he says he's thinking of going out West and getting a job. She's listening intently for my benefit, trying to make me listen intently by example to the fact that he's leaving. I want to tell her that I never forgot, but I won't. When Brandon goes, and Joey is already gone, we'll be sisters again, back to school, clasping each other's hands tightly.

I shouldn't think that. I should get no petty joy in thinking that once again we will be it for each other, back to back, Kate and Allie, Laverne and Shirley. I should tell her to fight for him. I should make him fight for her.

As then we all watch as Joey try to get into it with some boys on a nearby boat, four boys, shirtless Abercrombie models, all yelling at some imagined infraction. Stupid boys, but how could they know? They think that they're safe at four to one; they've never seen Joey kick someone until they vomited. They've never seen him with someone else's blood covering his face.

"No," Terran shouts and she gets up. She diffuses the situation with her beauty, one wave of the arm, one plea and the boys turn into grinning idiots and move off. A few whispered words to Joey and he spins, directing his familiar anger at her for the first time. I can see it take her breath away. Leach the steel from her spine.

"Not on my birthday, Joey," I say, maybe hurting more than helping, but I can't stand to see them look at each other like that. He smiles quickly at me.

"Sorry, Violet," he quickly responds, he apologizes to Terran too, and kisses her softly on the cheek. Then he shrugs out of her arms, goes for another beer, leaving her standing there. She stands there for a long time, her hair blazing around her face as the sun goes down behind us. When it's finally dark enough for the fireworks to begin, which are bound to be spectacular thanks to the rampant patriotism felt all over the nation, it's boys in the front and girls in the back. The boat is rocking softly, and none of us are very drunk anymore. The first blast goes off in a fizz of red, and I lean into Terran, sitting beside me.

"Men are bastards," she says softly, staring at Joey's back. She's been watching him for an hour as it got dark and he never once looked at her—this boy who used to follow her every move. She says the curse again under her breath and I frown. Women are always saying that, 'men are bastards.' I hold her around the shoulders as the fireworks go off, jubilant, exploding reaffirmations of America, colors flashing in the eyes of all of us watching.

Chapter 11

WE GO BACK WHILE COLORS ARE STILL POPPING IN THE SKY AND THE house is too quiet after all that noise. I take a quick shower and when I come out Brandon's alone in the den, watching TV.

"They've gone to bed?" I ask and he nods. He asks me if I want my birthday present. "Sure," I say. He smiles and we go back outside.

Joey's parents have a little, neglected two-person rowboat and that's what we take, whispering along the surface of the water. Brandon's rowing softly, his arms flexing and reaching underneath his T-shirt. The heat of the day is dissipating. The lake feels like a jar that's just had its lid pried off. I put my fingers into the exhausted water—water that's resting after being run through all day with motors and splashing legs.

Between us in the boat are cans of soda and a fresh pack of cigarettes. I can't help thinking of Terran and Joey, the image of him sliding out from underneath her hand is sticking with me, pasted up behind my eyes. When they smiled at each other today, their faces were the faces that you wear when you open up a cable-knit sweater on your 11th birthday. Brandon asks if I believe in soul mates. He's thinking of them too.

"Terran says that soul mates are just a lie that we tell ourselves." I replay that conversation that we had in the spare bedroom at Julia's party—that no one is special, and he snorts.

"Then what's she doing with Joey?"

Testing the theory maybe, I think, but instead I say, "What she does and what she says are two different things, these days."

"So what she's saying is that if you look for the ideal, you're setting yourself up for disappointment."

"Not necessarily. Love is all about how well you can lie to yourself. Believe the lie and it becomes the truth."

"To you, maybe," he says.

"Well, who else does it matter to?"

He looks at me with raised brows, his face different shades of blue and gray in the dark. The answer isn't good enough for him.

"Do you want to see what I got you for your birthday?"

I nod and he pulls a small black film container out of his pocket.

I smile. "You got me undeveloped naked pictures of yourself."

He grins, takes off the cap, then licks the tip of his finger and sticks it in. I open my mouth to receive it, the tiny slip of blotter acid dissolving on my tongue. He licks down his own and says, "Hey." He pulls me close, seals his mouth to mine carefully and this time his tongue is moving like his lips are moving, slow, sharing the drug. "Happy birthday," he whispers against me.

"If what Terran says is right, then that kiss was totally pointless," I say. I chew my hit into a ball and swallow it down. "Every kiss is the start of the clock, ticking away until you discover that everything special about the person you kissed you made up all on your own."

"Unless you can lie to yourself."

"Right." I feel my body lifted, grab onto the sides of the rowboat. But it's just the acid, coming up fast. I wonder if it was a good idea to go so far from shore.

Brandon shakes his head. "I don't know, Violet. I think that I have to keep kissing you. I think that I have to keep looking for that ideal." It's probably a doomed quest. But I don't say so. There's something a little bit beautiful about it, the idea of accepting nothing less than everything.

I touch his face in the dark and draw his mouth back to mine. It's all right if he wants to try it with me. Because we're running on a different clock. So I can kiss him and be safe. I can love him, and it could be perfect. But only because he's leaving.

I look up, my eyes starting to waver, and there are stars in the sky—too many to count, dazzling—so much better than in the city. I inhale and smell only air and remember the fireworks and the families and the happiness, kids writing their names with sparklers and parents trying to do the samba around the barbecue. Now in the dark I am consumed by this day. I am elated by its beauty and saddened as well—this glorious day that we cannot keep.

These are my last coherent thoughts. The acid has taken my mind, and I won't recover it until the dawn erupts in the east, as red as birth.

We're laying in the belly of the boat; I hear the water lapping behind my head. I think of all that darkness beneath me and all of the scaled, shimmering things in it and switch brain gears fast to something less creepy, my last chance to choose my topic before I go skittering down roads without directions, before I weave myself a great dripping web without logic.

I'm vaguely aware of Brandon at my side, but the trip is hard, too hard for another human to hold my interest. I can't stop thinking in fast lines and slow circles. My brain is overcome; it must bleed soon, be bled or burst, and I think loudly that this is what it must be like to know everything.

◆◆◆

The night of my actual birthday was made for lawn chairs. Long, comfortable lawn chairs set out on the beach and Terran and I are laid out like wilted flowers after the hot day. I can hear Terran's fingers tracing swirls in the sand next to me. There are so many bonfires that we have no need of our own, orange light flicks up to our right and left, competing music flaring and ebbing along with the glow. A few straggling fireworks go up over the lake in crackling white and pink. The sound is like a bomb as the color fades. Terran and I agree that we like the loud ones the best.

Most of the families are gone, packed up this morning in Range Rovers and sedans headed back to suburbia or the city. Now there is only leftover youth, getting drunk and loud. They are sixteen and some are 27, but somehow at 19 I feel like I should be slapping them on their backs and telling them it's time for bed. But I'm too lazy now. I smile and they drink on, tanned girls in bikini tops and shorts, dancing, flirting, and shouting. A beach-full of anonymous joy, and for just a second, I pretend that they're all celebrating my birthday.

Terran and Joey are fine again, one night is all it took. I hope that things are more than just patched. She bought me a cake this afternoon, lit all 19 candles and when I blew them out I thought I was going to burn my face off. We swam. The boys threw around a Frisbee. There was no talk of what was waiting for us at home. No talk of decisions, or the lack thereof.

Terran rolls her head to the side and smiles. "Happy Birthday, Violet. What do you want to do now?"

"Sleep, probably," I grin, the champagne in my belly agrees with me. A wet slurp on my toes startles me, and I look down. Between my feet is a medium-sized mongrel dog, with short black fur and white toes, and ears like fortune cookies. Terran kisses at it and it comes closer, squints its little eyes happily as she pets its head. Then it runs off.

Joey passes it on his way over and scratches its back before coming to stand between us, tells us to stop being lazy and grabs my ankles like he's going to pull me off of the chair.

Before I can object a sickening double-yelp erupts from our right, and Joey drops me.

There's more yelping, and a storm cloud of sand has been kicked up by someone's feet. The black mongrel dog is sliding along on its belly, circling and whining, its fortune cookie ears tucked tight against its head.

There's a big, ignorant boy walking slowly around the dog. He's got an expression on his face that says he isn't done yet, and I'm thinking, run you stupid dog, but maybe it can't. Maybe its legs are hurt or someone over there gave it some food, the little black thing that was all ribs, and now it won't go.

People are standing around watching, faces frozen in the firelight. No one moves to do anything. No one knows what provoked it, this ceaseless kicking of this animal. The dog is yelping, and the kid and his friends are laughing, the fear and pain they are inflicting on the animal is so funny. There's a whole crowd of us just staring. It's sick. I start to root for humanity and think that if he kicks that dog just once more, someone will make a move and that will be enough to get everyone moving—a shore full of people will save that dog.

I look over at Terran. She should really be the one to move, a beautiful advocate for mongrels, but she won't. She's thinking of Joey and her only goal is to keep him from a fight. She's got her hand up against his chest.

As it turns out, Brandon is the savior, coming in from nowhere, pushing the kid back, saving us from seeing that dog stomped to death or being scarred for life. His eyes are nothing but angry, and the terrified little dog is in the middle looking from one side to the other like it has to pick who gets to eat it.

"What is your problem?" he shouts at Brandon, "It's just a dog," as he looks at the dog and calls for a gun that one of his friends must have. He says that's going to shoot that dog, as he's moving toward it when Brandon moves fast and mean—hits him in the face with his fist and elbow.

No one tells them to take it easy. The fascination of the crowd has shifted from watching a dog be kicked to the possibility of seeing humans kick each other.

A couple of the kid's friends step off of the sidelines, but Joey is there to push them back into formation as the kid scrambles out of the dirt and goes for Brandon. The crowd is absolutely titillated by the rage, the idea that there might be blood. This might be a story to tell, but the kid stops short at the sound of a growl.

Everything stops at the sound of that growl. All eyes turn to that little dog still crouched in the sand, with all of its little white teeth showing.

Brandon's looking at it with admiration, all of the unflinching anger gone from his face. Then he claps his hands and laughs.

◆◆◆

"We'll be lucky if those guys don't burn this place down around our ears tonight," Terran says dismally, watching the black dog eat potato chips off of the kitchen floor. "Someone could have gotten really hurt, you know, and all over that stupid dog."

"It would have been worth it," Brandon says simply, flexing his hand and watching it swell.

"You really are Joey's cousin," I say before I get up to get a towel and ice. I can see that Terran isn't sure whether she should be pleased or pissed off about the comment. Joey only smiles.

I can hear them talking from down the hall as I pilfer through the linen closet. Terran's voice raising now and again and Brandon's staying maddeningly even. He tells her that he'd do it over again, that we all should have done it, and she interrupts, says that it's just a dog, and that's where they are when I walk back into the room. I take Brandon's hand from his lap so he can squeeze it on the ice pack.

"I don't like how you say that, 'it's just a dog, it's just a dog,' when there's nothing more evil than cruelty against an animal, nothing less sickening about mankind than the desire to stomp on something weaker, something innocent." Brandon proclaims coolly.

She rolls her eyes at him. "You talk about it like it's a child."

"It is a child. How are they different? In the face of that stupid kid, that dog had no more understanding than a child. It was helpless." Brandon retorted.

"It wasn't helpless. It growled, didn't it?" is Terran's reply.

Brandon smiles, a proud, almost secret smile, and I remember his laugh out there by the fire, his clapping, like he'd just found a roll of hundreds at the bottom of a Cracker Jack box.

"Look, my point is, it wasn't worth the risk," Terran says. "He probably wasn't going to kill that dog, but who knows what he might have done to you, or anyone else who got in the way. He was drunk; he might have broken that beer bottle and cut the shit out of you, and you'd have died for some stupid stray dog. Be practical."

"If I'd have died for that dog, I'd want it etched onto my headstone."

She looks at him and shakes her head, exasperated. "It's just a dog!"

"And we're just humans," I say. She looks at me sharply. Maybe she thinks that I'm only defending his point because we're together, and I guess we are together now, if so then it must totally escape her that she's most likely only arguing her point because Joey could have been dragged into the fray. She wanted to help that dog as much as anyone. She just didn't.

Brandon tugs me down on the couch and says, "That dog will follow me until she dies all because of one kind act. She'll never lie, or cheat, or beat someone up, or break someone's heart. Animals are everything that humans aren't."

"You think they're better," Terran says accusingly.

"Don't you think that humans are better?" Brandon says just as accusingly. "What makes my life, or yours, more valuable than hers?" We all turn to look at the little dog, lying next to the sofa now off to the side of Brandon's feet wagging her tail.

"Because we can value it," I say softly.

The next day we're packed into the SUV and that little black dog is riding shotgun, wedged into the seat with me and smiling her little dog grin as Brandon and Joey snore contentedly in the back. Brandon named the dog Penelope. Terran said that he should have named her Circe, as she seems to have a talent for turning men into pigs.

Now Terran's scratching Penelope underneath her chin, and behind her fortune cookie ears. Then she puts both hands back on the wheel and exhales, starts talking in monotone about her coming week, a Monday of headaches, a Tuesday of sweating and grinding her teeth, riding to work every morning with her mother trying to listen to the business news channel—her brain numbed by injections of ratios. By Thursday, she's a bundle of nerves. I laugh when she tells me that she's seriously considering early retirement in favor of alpaca farming.

But it's not that funny because part of her means it. Maybe most of her, no matter how easily that idea is identified as flawed. She can barely stand to talk about it. There's a vein standing out in her temple. The thought of her job makes her blood race, like tiny piranhas under her deceptively calm skin. She exhales again, and I can see her now, finally, see what she'd been trying to say to me up at the lake. She's tired. Far too tired for her 19 years. She's weary from walking a path tread by her mother's feet and millions of gray feet before hers.

But she'll be all right if she just stays with it. She'll rise to the top like cream, just like she's supposed to. She'll forget that there was ever anything else. And then she'll start to smile again, looking down and behind her at all of us staring up, a big crowd of us, envying and clapping.

It's late by the time Terran drops me off. I go into the house to find my father in a suit, pacing in the den. I kiss him hello and he asks how my birthday was, promises to take me out to dinner tomorrow night, but tonight they have to meet Bob and Sue Arnold. He asks why I smell like dog. I smile and go upstairs.

I watch my mother getting ready. She's got the bathroom door open and I'm leaning up against it, watching her be so careful with her makeup, careful not to smudge her dress. She looks perfect, she'd better, because she's going out tonight to be defined by other people. Everything in this world is at the mercy of the eyes upon it.

I can tell by the quick movements of her eyes and the half empty wine glass on the counter that she's already annoyed with my father. Her evening will end badly. She'll drink too much, and maybe she'll say something embarrassing about Bob Arnold's new wife. It'll make my father angry and the anger will make her sad, and she'll drink still more. They'll tread back and forth between expectation and disappointment, each act made laughable by the fact that this is what they've chosen.

"I thought you were going *out* for drinks," I say, looking at her glass she clicks her tongue at me and says that I wouldn't understand.

"You drink too much for your age," I say lightly. "Isn't that what *I'm* supposed to be doing?"

"You?" she says incredulously. "What in the world do YOU have to be drinking about?" I just shake my head. Then I tell her she wouldn't understand.

◆◆◆

Downtown smells like steel and sulfur today. No telling where the smells are coming from, they drift around the corners of buildings in half a million fingers, the scent just as strong as its source. I'm walking in a crowd, everyone keeping polite distance, that 5-inch bubble of personal space, but they're still making me walk fast on a Saturday. Even faster than on a workday because their leisure time is so much more scarce and valuable.

I slow down intentionally and feel the hate from the people behind me, people who almost run up against me and breach the bubble. They'd like to curse at me and tell me to get out of the way, they've got things to do. I'd like to tell them to calm down, that they've got another sixty years to live, maybe more with modern medicine. I want to ask why it is that those extra years don't amount to extra time. But they're gone before I can open my mouth, up ahead of me and crossing the street, with their muscular legs and racing hearts, trying to catch up with their heads, which are already waiting for them somewhere else. They remind me of that game I used to play as a kid, where the goal of plastic animals was to grab as many white marbles as you could. I can't think of it.

Hungry Hungry Hippos. I watch them go past me, still cursing under their breaths, shooting disgusted looks at me, talking about my rudeness to their friends even though I only cost them a second. Half a second. I'm contrasted with them sharply, and the contrast makes me smile.

I get to the record store long after the people I was walking with have reached their destinations. I call it the record store because they have a section of old vinyl, in the back, behind a long velvet curtain, hiding it like the 18+ room in a video store. I don't go in there. As much as I am fond of those nostalgic old dusty jackets, so much more interesting than the cracking plastic of CD cases come on, who still has a record player?

Today I'm looking for some Ani DiFranco, To the Teeth maybe, or Living in Clip, something political and outspoken to at least flow through my head even if it will never come out of my mouth. I know the way, reverse alphabetical order to the rear of the store, past the "tobacco" pipes and incense, straight past Tenacious D, PJ Harvey, and G. Love. I just start flipping through the cases, assembled in plastic crates, when I hear a laugh. It's Joey's laugh.

I could have heard Joey talking for minutes on end without recognizing his voice. But his laugh snaps me straight upright. The laugh of a friend is more notable than his voice alone; it catches the ear much easier, easier even than an overheard whisper. It's conspiratorial in its unshared joy.

He's behind the curtain, back in the vinyl section, and of course my first impulse is to let him be. That laugh was not for me, and no matter what kind of friends we are, my emergence into the record section would only cause a halt to the laughter. Probably even an awkward pause.

So I keep flipping through Ani, through four copies of Puddle Dive; he'll see me when he comes out. I wait. Patient until I hear the answering giggle. It's a girl giggle. A flirtatious girl giggle that doesn't belong to Terran.

His words are in my ears again, 'we're inseparable,' and so is the look on his face when he said it. Friendship requires that I pull back the curtain.

Joey and Julia look up from where they stand near the first row, their faces more than surprised, and the ensuing silence is more than awkward. She's got her fingers looped through his belt. Even though I'm staring at them she doesn't pull them out. She leans forward, whispers something in his ear and he smiles, a reluctant smile, the can't-help-myself smile. She goes to leave and says, "Hey Violet," as she passes. I let the curtain fall shut behind her I then pull it back open, watching her go. I don't care when she looks back to see if I'm watching.

"Hey," Joey says, flipping through CCR albums. I walk up to him, close. I say, "You don't have a record player."

"Gift for Brandon," he says. It's a pretty good cover. Brandon likes CCR and he is the type to have a record player somewhere. As Joey talks the lie gets better and better, like that's where all of his wit is stored. In the lying part of his brain. "We got into this debate about Fogerty yesterday, CCR versus post-CCR and I thought—"

"What are you doing?" I ask, and he stops in mid-sentence.

"I don't know," he responds.

I gave up finding any on the music and let Joey drive me home. Now I'm contemplating calling Terran. I even pick up the phone. If it were nothing, I would call. I would call just for something to do, just to stir up some trouble, to give her the heads up and prove my loyalty. But I don't think that it is nothing, and for some reason that shuts me up, even though I know it's unwise, to be Joey's secret-keeper. He'll undoubtedly tell her and she'll know that I knew.

I feel the guilt for betraying her even though I can't really believe he's guilty of anything. Not with Julia, that vapid, superficial redhead, who is nothing special compared to Terran. All of these thoughts are spinning in my head, and my control of them is giving way to melodrama and suspicion, so I'm not exactly ready for what awaits me in the den.

"Violet," I hear my father call out and when I look up I think 'what now,' because he's forcing a smile that says he wishes I weren't dressed like such a hood, even though it's only khakis a tank and a bag slung over my shoulder. "I'd like you to meet someone."

There's an old man sitting on my parents' sofa, beside my mother. Of course he would hesitate to call himself old, he can't really be over 55, but he's clearly older than my parents and to me that makes him practically dead. He's wearing glasses, and his skin is worn but still golden. His hair is starkly white.

Everyone stands and I shed my bag to take the outstretched hand. My father introduces him as Dr. Collins. Doctor. You've got to be kidding me. I'm nineteen years old and being mentored in my parents' living room.

As it turns out, the old Doctor is a good friend (read client) of my father's. As it also turns out, he's heard a lot about me. He talks to me at length regarding his profession (he's a rheumatologist in with a private practice), I ask the right questions, leading him forward, toward the end of the speech, with enough head nods and laughing to keep everyone engaged as he romanticizes the art of diagnosis.

"And the best part is," he says, in his voice that is so free of any accent that I know he's worked hard to lose it, "I help people." Pride rushes out in those words, knocking us all back in our chairs to be impressed. Then it pulls back into his chest and we rock back forward.

"And did you always want to be a rheumatologist?" I ask.

"Pardon me?" he replies looking surprised.

"Even when you were a little boy, did you want to be a rheumatologist? Was it your dream?" He looks at me quizzically. Then he looks at my father, unsure of whether this question about his youth is a sign of piqued interest or just inappropriate.

"Well," he says finally, breaking eye contact and rubbing his hands along his knees. "Little boys dream of being Superman!" We all laugh. "Little boys dream of going on safari and exploring the wilds of the Amazon. Of being secret agents or maverick paleontologists." He chuckles. "Silly, little boy dreams." He's trailing off and I wait patiently, wanting to be respectful of the silly dreams of a rheumatologist.

"And why rheumatology?" I ask. "Why not pediatrics, or the ER?"

"Well that's easy! There are so few of us rheumatologists, you know. Often overlooked but a lucrative area to specialize in. I had my own practice in a matter of years! It was the obvious choice." He replied excitedly.

My father is nodding along, so excited and impressed that I feel like the worst kind of slacker for not being excited and impressed. I'm careful to keep my eyebrows raised; I'm careful to nod, because I don't want that happy expression on my father's face to fade. Even my mother is wearing a pleased cat's smile, although I'm sure she's not imagining me as a rheumatologist. More likely some kind of a surgeon.

I look at Dr. Collins and for a moment I see a little boy with a blanket wrapped around his shoulders like a cape. I look at my mother and see the girl with the flushed cheeks and her hands clenched in righteous fists. Then my father puts an arm around me that looks confident but feels awkward and I see the doctor again, the old man, grinning and nodding; I see my mother, made-up and nervous. They want me to see their point. They want me to be like them, and odds are that I will be, someday. But just now I can't. Not here, with my father's Leave-it-to-Beaver arm around my shoulder. Here I can only look and wonder at their smiles, wonder how the fuck they can pretend to be pleased with what's happened to them, and how they've convinced themselves that they mean it."It's a noble profession," my father says to me, snapping me back into the conversation. "Nobody can look down on a doctor."

Dr. Collins chuckles and stands, says that he should be getting back but that it was a lovely afternoon. We accompany him to the door.

No one looks down on a doctor, is what my father said, and now I know what rheumatology is. Now I know what success is. It is aspirin for life, a great relief from the pain of peoples' eyes constantly bearing down on you. "Focus hard on your undergrad," Dr. Collins says to me on his way out. "But don't feel too pressured. I'd be happy to put in a word or two with the admissions board at my alma mater. And I have good relations with colleagues on several other boards as well."

"Thank you, Dr. Collins," I say shaking his hand one more time. My father claps me on the back, so excited, all his hopes projected onto me. When I lean into my mother I'm so heavy it's a wonder that I don't knock her over.

◆◆◆

We're sitting on the rocks in a circle and there's a joint going around. It's a nice night, just enough of a breeze to keep the bugs off and the heat is breaking up. I'm worried about the girl with the dead eyes sitting across from me who used to be Terran; I want to kick her into the stream just to wake her up. I told her about my encounter with Dr. Collins and everything I thought it meant, but she wasn't really listening. She doesn't really listen anymore, not like she used to. Her ears are already too stuffed with voices of her own.

She'll be all right. I can tell by the way she smiles at me sometimes, a soft, closed-lip smile that says she's okay, she's just tired; she's okay, she's just sad. Now and then I'll say something encouraging, try to let her know that she doesn't have that much farther to go, that her path is paved already. She just has to swim a little more, kick through a few more sets of eyes before she breaks the surface and then she'll be lifted out, weightless. She smirks when I say these things. Smirks and looks straight into my eyes, like she's looking into a mirror. The joint is miniscule now and gets tossed into the river—a sticky offering for the undines.

As we smoke and talk, we pay no attention to Brandon and Joey, and they've filled the space left by our neglect with stories of other girls. They're laughing on the heels of something that Joey said about having sex in his mother's car and her being horrified to find the condom in the backseat the next day. He goes on to say that the girl was the biggest nymphomaniac he's ever met—that she wanted it everywhere—the car, the bed, the floor, against the wall. Brandon's face is pure admiration. Terran puts her hand on Joey's knee and his story cuts off suddenly, like he'd just remembered that she was sitting there. She stops him with her hand and I stop Brandon with my eyes. We can't bear to hear any more. Not because we're overtly jealous. Not because the story is vulgar, although it undoubtedly is. But because a lover's past is not to be borne. It's why Terran has never mentioned her boyfriend at college, why I don't talk about Brian, and why Brandon skirts the subject of the parade of girls he's surely had. Every love had in the past is a betrayal of the love of the present. It says that this love is not special, that you are only one of many. The past must be stomped out and forgotten, as evidence that nothing is as important as you, as now. Or it must be made tolerable by breaking it up into less significant bits. We use phrases like, "I never really loved them," or, "I've never felt this way about anyone else." Usually lies, of course, but lies that even the speaker believes, because the victory of present over past is not only vital to one lover, but to both.

The sky is getting dark and the moon is small. We have to go soon or we'll break our ankles on unseen roots. Brandon is off of the rocks first.

"I don't want to go home," Terran says, looking up at me quickly, and then at the guys as well. "What do you say?"

She brings us into the city, wanting to dance until she sweats, hopping us from club to club like rave kids who know the scene, until she finds one that's loud enough, that's blue enough, one with enough strobe to give any dancer the illusion of rhythm. She slides onto the dance floor with Joey and we're right behind them, Brandon puts his lips to my ear and says that he wants me, electrifying little phrase, validating little phrase from a boy who is every inch as handsome as Joey though with little resemblance—the rock star to Joey's Ralph Lauren.

I kiss him and he's got his hands on me; I whisper into his ear "maybe," even though there's enough lust in my thighs to fuel an orgy. Maybe it's just the weed, but it feels better than anything before, better than Brian, better than the boy in high school with the expert tongue; it's lust that doesn't just stop at my hips. Or maybe that's just Violet-In-Love talking. Or even worse, Stoned-Violet-In-Love. I've lost track of Terran. It's late; she'll want a hotel room soon, she meant what she said about not going home. My eyes find them, dancing safely, close together, Terran looking intent on thinking of nothing but dancing, and Joey staring up toward the second level. I follow his gaze and see that the object of his fascination is a slim girl in a tube top with bright red hair.

Chapter 12

Terran booked adjoining rooms at the Marriott and we're in the elevator. I'm watching Terran and Joey grope each other like they're trying to live out an old Aerosmith video. I'm as voyeuristic as anyone else, but the charm fades when the people are your best friends and you know that you're going to have to listen to their banging headboard all night long.

Brandon reaches out and grabs Terran by the hips, pulls her off of Joey and into his arms where she squeals, a little drunk and pretty stoned, and then we're at our floor. Terran and Joey walk out and promptly resume kissing, but Brandon hangs back, and takes me by the arm. He tells them we're going out for a walk.

"I don't feel like walking," I say, reaching toward the buttons.

"I don't either," he says, and tosses the keys to Terran's Mercedes up into the air, then catches them with one hand. He must have lifted them off of her when he had her in his arms. I call him a delinquent.

"Useful delinquent," he corrects me. "Let's get out of the city."

Outside is the nighttime city, deceptively still, no merging, no honking, no stress, disturbing in its dissimilarity to itself. I lift my head out of my body and up into the sky, where I can look down on it and see it for real, see all of the headlights still crawling through the streets, see the city still seethe like an open wound.

Brandon's driving, pushing the Mercedes along at its usual 80, and soon enough the city lights are dying behind us, hazy glow thrown up into the sky like a yellow brick road. I know Terran will be mad tomorrow when she finds out that her car didn't stay put, but she'll be even more mad when I tell her that Brandon was behind the wheel. I don't care. I don't care because back in the hotel room she's screwing Joey with the ardor of a bride on her wedding night while he closes his eyes and pretends that her blonde hair is red. I don't care because beyond the smog of the city there are stars.

Before long there are signs naming rivers and we pull off to go find one, park the SUV and follow our noses and ears to the oil-black water. Brandon asks me what I'm thinking after a few minutes of standing. I tell him I'm thinking about Terran and Joey. I recount the scene from the record store and again I'm an asshole for telling Brandon and not her.

"Is he cheating on her?" I ask.

"If he's not already then he will be soon," he says, and shrugs. But maybe he already is, and that's the best answer that Brandon can give me without breaking the guy-code of honor. I'm smoldering in my skin, thinking of Julia, our false friend, all green eyes and white skin, no freckles. She's a lucky redhead. She must be so proud of her conquest; because anything stolen is all profit, and anything stolen from Terran automatically doubles in value.

I think of her smile when she greets Terran at parties. I think of her old dislike for Joey. It was only Terran's interest in him that made him worth taking.

I hate her, quick simple hate, knee-jerk hate, and it comes easy because she has no loyalty. Because she's broken Terran's girl-code. Terran's stupid girl-code, because there is no girl-code. There is no honor among thieves with spread legs.

Terran. There's nothing I can do to help her, so my mind pulls back and blames her, because I refuse to berate Joey right now. It would only pit me against Brandon in a useless fight between bitches and bastards. It's the oldest struggle in the world, and one that will never be won. "She's an idiot."

"Who?"

"Terran," I say I can feel his smirk in the dark, hear it in the scoffing exhale through his nose. "What? She's an idiot for loving him. It's making her blind."

"Like that old saying, 'True love is blind'?" I shake my head, because that phrase is moronic. If I had written it, I'd have left out the 'True' altogether. "She can't help who she loves," he says.

"That's ridiculous. She doesn't even believe that herself, remember? Nobody has to love anybody."

"Our parents love us because they have to. It's biological."

"The biological instinct is protection. Promulgation of the species. Love is something different—something beyond that. Love is a choice. It's only human self-justification that makes us think otherwise. We all use love as an excuse for stupid decision making."

He rubs my shoulders and I let him do it. I hate to be at odds with love, letting the cynic inside me strangle the poet, the cynic so angry and the anger derived from fear, the fear that humanity has lost the ability to love. That love isn't a real word anymore, just a composite name given to all of our own desires, our own needs, to be wanted, to be special, to be excited. That love is something that is done to us.

"Let's say you're right," he says, dropping his arms from my shoulders and despite my hard talk, the absence of his touch makes me cold. "That love is a choice." He stands beside me and throws something into the water. "It's still a choice that I'll always make the same way.

"You think that Terran being in love with Joey makes her stupid. That it makes her less than what she normally is, but I say that it makes her more. Only when we're in love do we ever really put someone else ahead of ourselves, and in doing so the person in love becomes a person to love. Worthy of love. Sometimes it's tragic, but it's always heroic. When we're in love we get to live out our own fantasies of ourselves."

I let his words sink in. I know that's how Terran must see herself now, as noble, the ultimate woman, every sacrifice a gift and every gift a private joy. But Joey's weakness for red hair will make her feel her stupidity soon enough. I know that I can't save her from that and part of me doesn't want to; it's too easy for me to judge because I'm suspended above them, having never been this kind of stupid.

Brandon's hands are on my waist. He still wants what he's been wanting all night. His mouth opens mine and he pushes forward, pushing with his tongue and pressing me close with his hands, making me taut, turning me into a bow and he whispers, "I love you, Violet."

"I love you, Brandon," I say, which is stupid after what I've just said, but I don't have to. I don't have to love him. Except that feels like it might be a load of shit as he slides his hand between my thighs and we lower ourselves to the ground and take each other, my hands clutching his back, his lips praying to my neck.

The liar in me screams out that this is like nothing else, and I know that I'll never tell him what I really suspect about love. That it has a shelf-life here, that it can't survive in all of this piss, in all of these bitches and dirt and details. I'll never tell him that. Not unless he promises to never believe me.

◆◆◆

Over the next week I thought that things might have gone back to normal, back to what they should be, because I didn't hear from anyone but Brandon, when we would get together at night to drink, or to make love. Make love. I've never been able to use that phrase out loud and keep a straight face. Love. Is that what we're making when we're sweating and groaning and invading each other? Is that what women are brewing up in their bellies, what men have boiling down in their pants? Once upon a time maybe. In fairy stories, where the prince and princess fucked into the wild blue yonder and never wanted to "make" anything with anybody else.

During the day I've been online, pulling up Web sites and essays and encyclopedia entries, snippets of everything from Accounting to Zoology. At first I really thought I was onto something; bits about aeronautics and botany and cultural studies were interesting. But only bits. No gravitating spark, nothing to make me do anything but say "hmm" very thoughtfully. I suppose it doesn't really matter anyway. Anything I choose is ultimately settling; it'll be the shrug that I give when I realize that I can't be a movie star or the front man for a rock 'n roll band.

It's silly of me to think that way, because I'm a person, and people have a real tendency to settle, and settle well; they can change whatever it is that they've stumbled into, they can turn it into a dream, as long as there's any hope that they'll succeed. Maybe that's more practical. It's certainly more sensible than beating themselves senseless against an ivory rock.

In front of me on the breakfast table is a trade magazine featuring today's candidate: several articles on bioengineering and cloning. But there's something downright creepy about growing a sheep out of a tube that's the same sheep as another sheep but separate. Besides, my father gave a derisive little snort when he saw me reading it.

But he's gone now, off for 18 holes with Nick Durso, one of the partners, so I can read all about the dual sheep, and the pros and cons of stem cell research, and a myriad of other things that are far too smart for me—far too smart for most of us, really. Seventy-eight percent of the population considers themselves to be of above average intelligence. Do the math, people.

My mother gestures toward my cell phone. I didn't even hear it ring. She makes a face at my magazine and says that she wishes I wouldn't read that sort of thing at the breakfast table. I suppose images of cell research and internal shots of cancer patients aggravate her hangover. I answer my phone.

"Violet?" Comes Joey's voice, plaintive through the tiny holes.

I say "Hey Joey, how have you been?" he replies quickly "okay." He starts telling me what's been going on, that somebody dented his passenger side door and didn't leave a note, that Penelope the dog peed all over his mother's kitchen floor, that Brandon talks about me a lot. "How's Terran?" I ask and I can hear it even through the phone. He shuts up so fast, sucks himself in and holds it, like those sea anemones on the Discovery Channel do when a diver touches them. "Working a lot, I suppose," I say to help him along.

"Yeah."

"Or maybe still snubbing me for taking her car without permission?"

"Maybe," he says, and then, "No, probably not."

I'm beginning to wonder why he called. I just want to read about doubling and tripling sheep. I want to feel some cloned wool.

"Well," I say, grinning wide so that the sound of the grin will carry through the phone, "Butter her up for me just in case.

We've got to go back up to school soon, and I don't want to get left here."

He ignores it like it wasn't even said, and anxiously asks me what I'm doing this weekend.

"I don't know, probably nothing." He suggests that Terran and I hang out. I can tell that it really is his suggestion this time; he's not just being her little message boy. He lays out our Saturday for us in one long, pre-planned breath, his voice the worst kind of forced nonchalant, and he's a bad actor too.

I exhale, flip my magazine shut, and say, "Joey, you shit."

"What? She'll need something to do; she hates to be by herself on the weekends, it's the only time she gets away. I know she'd really like some time with you," he says. It's no wonder he called, because I would have given him the finger or broken something over his head by now if he were standing in front of me.

"Look," he says, getting desperate because I'm not cooperating, "I'm going to be over at Fischer Park by noon, so I can't take her out." He's not subtle. Fischer Park is an overgrown wildlife preserve where all of the jocks used to go to do the cheerleaders in high school. Julia will know it well.

"Why are you telling me this?" I ask quietly.

He's silent for so long, but I'm going to give him a 10 count before I scream his ears off and call him a chicken shit bastard.

"Why," I say once more—last chance, and he says,

"I'm sorry, Violet," and then I know. After I hang up on him, my mother casually slides a stack of pancakes onto the table in front of me, not meeting my eyes, pretending that making pancakes is an intense enough activity to keep her from listening to my phone conversation. But then curiosity gets the better of her.

"What was that all about, Violet? That was Joey, wasn't it?"

"It was nothing, Mom," I mumble, and then, suddenly too weary to keep secrets, "Just that Joey is going to cheat on Terran this weekend with a friend of ours and I've been recruited to show her."

"What?"

"Why do we even make breakfast anyway? You don't eat it, and I don't like it, so what's the deal? Why don't we just start the day with pizza?"

"Because that wouldn't be normal," she says, sipping a mimosa and scrubbing at imagined dirt on the marble countertop.

"Normal is overrated," I quip, staring at the tower of dough steaming before me. Normal is synonymous with boring; it's one step over from ordinary.

I'm tired. Joey has trapped me. I know what he's going to do; I'm too certain of it to be able to convince myself that I could leave her in the dark with a clear conscience, afraid of being wrong. Unless I burn my 'good friend' hat between now and Saturday, I'll be taking her out shopping. And then to lunch. And then to catch her boyfriend screwing someone else. I just woke up an hour ago and already I could go back to sleep. The heat from the pancakes is suddenly so comforting that I butter them, and even put on some syrup. But in the end I just sit there, with my fork stabbed in, protruding from the center like a bizarre sundial—like an empty flagpole.

◆◆◆

Saturday comes sooner than I want it to, and at the last minute I find that I can't stand the pretenses. Bitch that I am for doing it his way, out of all of the other ways I could do it, and I can't stomach the pretenses of shopping and lunch. So I call her and tell her to wait for me, and now I'm making the walk to her mother's house—a long walk—and she didn't offer to pick me up.

I haven't made this walk since we were young, before cars and speed, warm days when I would say that I was coming over and then show up an hour and a half later. But this is no warm day. It's nearly noon and the sun is baking my pale shoulders. I'll have tank strap-lines before the hike is over, bright white against bright pink, which will fade to an angry red and then right back to white again, passing over tan entirely—like that Robert Frost poem. The beads of sweat on my forehead say that I should have gotten a car this summer, or at least ridden a bike, but I'm too old now for pleasure-biking; I can't just pedal along anymore without feeling absurdly like one of the Doublemint Twins.

I see through my squinting eyes that Terran's mother's house is looming up ahead on the hill, big, so I know it's still far away. If I were close it would be enormous. But there's no time for breaks. No time for thinking, not about why I'm doing it his way, why I'm not just sitting her down and telling her gently. Why I'm showing her instead. Why I'm not forcing him to tell her himself.

Maybe it's because I still can't stand them shutting me out. Maybe I want to be involved. Maybe it's because I don't want either of them to be able to wriggle out of it. This way there can't be any excuses, no chance for a lie-riddled reconciliation. Maybe I just want to hold their eyes open and scream that this is the truth. But those ugly thoughts are my own truth, my own pallid face reflected back at me in a smoked mirror. I'm utterly ridiculous. I refuse to rubberneck when I'm passing car crash sites just to make a point. I sentimentalize road kill just to make a point. And what point is that? Because I am above nothing; I am no different than any leering crowd. I push my legs into longer strides so that maybe I won't have the energy to keep Psych 101-ing myself. And also because I have to hurry. I can't expect Joey and Julia to wait around all day screwing.

"I'm glad you called," she says to me across the kitchen counter as I slurp ice water. "I need to talk to you."

"Listen, I'm sorry about taking your car the other night. It was stupid and inconsiderate." She tells me not to worry about it. I haven't been. I just need to apologize for something. She's smiling at me perfectly, not a bit distracted by Joey's absence, just glad that I'm here. I think for a second fuck Joey, let him pointlessly screw Julia all day if he wants to.

I sip again at the ice water—delicious—poured straight from a bottle. I hate talking in this house, anywhere besides Terran's bedroom. I hate thinking here. It always seems that I can feel Meredith rising up behind me, all piercing eyes and stretched smile. That Meredith's house pulls in closer whenever we whisper.

"I really need to talk to you about something," Terran says again. I say sure, why don't we go talk at Fischer Park, where we'll never get to talk about anything, because something more pressing will come up. She gives me a weird look, kind of teasing, like I'm taking her up there to get into her pants, but she says okay. But when we get out into her SUV, she hesitates after half-turning the key in the ignition.

"Maybe not Fischer Park," she says staring at the wheel. "Why not just drive, you know, drive until we find some place nice to stop." She sounds almost scared. But she can't know. Maybe she just suspects, and if that's true, then I can't lead her into it blind. I feel like Clytemnestra on the red carpet, only she had the vengeance of Iphigenia to hold up her duplicitous smile. I don't.

"It has to be Fischer Park," I say simply. "Because Joey's there."

On the way to Fischer Park I tell her everything, in a deliberate monotone to keep my guilt around my neck. I won't be unburdened by my own desperate, gossipy voice.

"I'm sorry," I say, but it doesn't sound anything like sorry; it sounds like I've been on stage reading bad poetry.

To her credit she says nothing. No questions, no tearful expressions from her mouth or on her face. Just a steady stare out through the windshield—her mother's stare. We park right behind Joey's red Mitsubishi, and I mentally picture a horrifying fallout, Terran flipping and pulling a Towanda on the rear end of his car before we drive away. We get out and start walking. No point in driving out here and then missing the show.

"He's probably this way," I say, and she stays just off my shoulder. We pick through shrubs and shiny weeds and I hope that Julia gets, literally, a fucking rash. Terran, mind reader, pulls me past some poison oak. We stay close to the trees, covert. She knows what's happening, but I still feel like the worst kind of bitch. I'm giving him what he wants. I'm ending it for him, this wonderful thing that he's chased after for his entire adult life, and I'm ending it in a way that suits his taste, violent and hysterical. An end that can't be escaped or rationalized.

I catch sight of them around a little bend and hold Terran back in the cover. They're not fucking yet but they're close, up against the rocks, standing up, and it's a total show. They could have taken the ground, or the bench, either one would have been more practical, more comfortable, but not as dramatic, and that's what matters. Putting on a show. Julia keeping her eyes open, to see the look on Terran's face.

I watch Terran carefully to see if something's going to crack behind her irises. I can hear Joey and Julia, rustling and moaning and where are the park rangers? Where are the cops? Minutes go by with Terran just watching, unblinking and expressionless. I wonder what kind of plan is hatching behind those unfocused eyes.

But it seems that they'll just keep fucking on display for an attack that isn't going to come. Because Terran's pulling me back quietly, her face as still as it has been since I told her where Joey was. She'll give them nothing. On the drive back she stops once and vomits. She lets the SUV idle and holds my hand tight, looking at nothing and weighing my arm down. I brush some damp strands of hair away from her eyes. It's a good thing that she doesn't believe in soul mates.

Chapter 13

It's been 3 days since Joey made his performance art split with Terran—since she dropped me off in my driveway, smiled at me, and kissed my hand. If she blames me at all, then she's hiding it well. She's hiding everything well. She called me yesterday from the restroom on her lunch break and the entire conversation was about me. Not one word about Joey. Nothing about Julia. Nothing about work. For a mad second, I thought maybe they'd worked it out and gotten back together. But Brandon says no, that Joey has started bringing Julia to the house.

So I'm a little bit surprised and a little bit relieved when I see Joey's Mitsubishi pull into my parents' driveway. I half-smile at his tinted windows and too-loud radio. I call him on his cell and tell him to turn it down before I get in, a stupid little thing we used to do in high school. Now it's a nostalgic gesture meant to cement us together. He takes me to the park. Not Fischer Park, but a real one, with swings and slides.

"Listen, I'm sorry I did that to you," he says. I shrug. I'd been daydreaming about myself as a World War II Red Cross Nurse in the car and I'm not out of it yet. It's hot, and bright, and we must look terribly cool in our dark sunglasses, because nobody meets our eyes as we walk the paved path, none of the kids run up to us to show us their sand piles made from red plastic buckets, and even joggers yield, swerving around us onto the grass. I glance over at Joey, his head cocked down, black hair sucking up the light, hands thrust into his pockets. I stop and he stops.

"Why did you do it, Joey?"

He shrugs and looks at his feet, mumbles something like, "because I'm an asshole," and I poke him in the chest with my finger.

"Look, it sounds stupid," he begins. I tell him that what he did was stupid so not to worry about the stupidity of the explanation. He starts to walk again and we climb up onto a picnic table, sit on top with our feet on the benches and watch the kids swing. They go higher and higher, pumping their little legs, throwing their bodies into it and sending the swing crooked with their lack of control. Then they jump off, and squeal before they hit the sand and scream, "Mommy, my ankle!" before catching the pendulum and doing it again. They are thrill seekers with long days.

"I still want her," Joey says quietly, still watching the kids.

"Then why are you messing around with Julia?" I ask, my voice carefully toneless.

He shakes his head. "I don't know," he says and laughs. "I don't even like her that much. Actually I don't like her at all." I want to pull off his sunglasses to see if he's high. "I still want Terran."

"I don't get it." I can see him struggling with his limited vocabulary. Whatever he says, it will be up to me to read between the inarticulate lines.

"I don't either," he says. "I need to want her. I thought I needed to get her, but—"

I wait for him to say that she didn't live up to his fantasy, to his own fairy tale expectations. He doesn't.

"I couldn't stand to have her. It was like dying," he says finally and shakes his head, unsatisfied, the words not exactly right. After a few more attempts to exorcise the thoughts from his tongue, a few feeble gestures from his hands, he gives up. I lean against him on the picnic table, shifting closer on the peeling brown paint.

I think that I might understand. I think Joey wanted Terran for too long. There wasn't anything left of him besides the wanting and to have her was like being snuffed out. He's blameless really, because this is how we live, one foot down in front of the other in one long march of wanting—that hunger keeping us moving—so that we can never be content. We forget our triumphs, no matter how golden; we leave them in the sand for others to see while we move forward toward that new thing behind the glass: a car, a girl, a job.

"So," he says, throwing his arm around my shoulders, "How's that decision of yours coming along?" I shrug and tell him that it's not, not really, and he says that I shouldn't be embarrassed. That I shouldn't let anyone tell me it's a light decision to make.

"Was it easy for you to pick psychology?" I ask him.

He looks out at those kids, still swinging and screaming, making up games for themselves that no one else knows the rules to. "You know they say that the world is out in front of you like some kind of buffet," he says, "but it's not. Not for us. Not even for Terran, although she's got the best shot at it." He smiles and it looks menacing behind his sunglasses. That's how Joey will always be. Sad and angry. Pretty and menacing. "I can't be an archaeologist, Violet. I can't be an architect, or a neurosurgeon. Even in the military I'm no Navy Seal. No special ops. I'm a foot soldier. So was it easy to pick psych? Sure. But only because it seemed like the best option out of three. Something worth paying a hundred grand for that I could actually pull off."

"The glass ceilings of our heads," I say, and he looks at me, puzzled, so I smile and say, "Never mind." I look up at those kids, grinning youth, their faces red with excitement and exertion, thinking of nothing but fun, their bellies full to fatness with macaroni and cheese. I don't know whether to envy them or pity them, but I always hope for them. "So what are you going to do with that psych degree, Joe?"

He doesn't really answer. He just smiles his cutting smile and shrugs. "Three years 'til then," he says and looks down at his shoes. I think that he'll do this every summer, this little ritual of coming to terms with the fact that another year has gone by with him still alive. He looks at me suddenly. "I thought I might go to the city to see that thing. That 9/11 thing, you know, the two lasers in the sky. The Towers of Light."

"They took that down."

"Oh," he says, disappointed. "That sucks. It seemed really—." He looks up at the kids again. "Important."

"Yeah," I mumble, looking at the kids as well but thinking of what that tribute must have looked like up close, all of that light where there used to be steel, twin beams shot up into the sky, like two phantoms for our memory. Right in the city, and it's hard to believe that nothing made of steel will ever be there again.

But I suppose that 'ever' is only two or three lifetimes from now. Two hundred years and the deaths will have lost their meanings, will only be taught in textbooks, and something new will spider up in that lucrative space. I wonder about the milestone of those two planes, if it will become a divider for two eras, pre-9/11 and post-9/11. A nation defined by an event. I almost hope not. I don't really want to be living in anything that could be called an aftermath, like there's nothing left to see but ashes.

"Brandon's talking about leaving," he says quietly.

I smile. "I was wondering when he was going to start that." He hasn't mentioned a thing to me, so I know that he'll be going soon, in the only kind of departure that suits him. Spontaneous and fast. Joey's relieved by my non-reaction; I don't think he wanted to comfort me today. But I know what it meant for him to tell me, so I thank him and lean my head against his shoulder.

"You know, Violet," he says, "Next year, when we come back here again, things won't be the same." I hear that voice of his, simple and resolute; I feel the weight of his arm.

"Oh, Joey," I sigh. "They aren't the same now." And really, who would want them to be?

◆◆◆

Brandon and I are walking Penelope, sweeping a path for us on the sidewalk with her nose. He still hasn't told me when he's leaving, or that he's even thinking about it. I'm not really expecting him to. We turn a corner and now we're on the street with the deli, and the owner, or now I assume that he's the owner, is out again, broom in hand, stirring up little storms of dirt and debris as he pushes it toward the curb and gutter. Penelope tries to sniff him and he jumps a little, glances up at us for reassurance. When he gets it he looks slightly annoyed. There was no recognition in his face for me. Why should there be? Why do I keep having this notion that one day he'll know me, that when I walk by he'll smile and I'll smile back—that maybe we'll even know each other's first names. I don't know. We aren't friends; he's just a symbol, and I'm just a symbol. As we pass I hear the scrape of his broom on the ground. It doesn't seem charming or quaint anymore, not like it did on that lazy afternoon when the street was breezy and deserted. Now it feels like a chore, the scrape scrape scrape in his ears every day, and I suddenly want a broom in my hands too, to be united with him in the common experience of insignificant things.

Two more corners turned and we're back at Brandon's car. We creak the doors open and Penelope jumps into the backseat with her leash still on; I don't know how she can stand it. The heat flowing out of the interior is enough to make the air go hazy.

"I'm leaving," Brandon says suddenly.

"Out West?" I say, because I can't think of anything else. I duck into the hot Chevy.

"I guess," he says, once he's behind the wheel. He starts the engine and we roll down the windows. Penelope's pink tongue is next to my ear immediately, trying to get her head out.

"I want you to come with me."

"What?"

He flashes a smile. Full of mischief and ideas. "Come with me. Forget school for now; send your dad a postcard. You can bankroll our Kerouac adventure."

I laugh. I've just heard Brandon's version of a sales pitch; no matter what he'd like me to think I know it wasn't spontaneous, he's been mulling it over for days, maybe weeks, whether or not he should take on a passenger. I let myself think about it, for a few long seconds, the role that he's cast me in. I'm the bored, confused rich girl that he sweeps up and teaches how to scream. I'm grateful to be part of his fantasy. But people's fantasies rarely match. He hasn't looked at me since he brought it up. I don't even know when we'd leave, he'd likely just pull into my driveway one night and ask if I needed a few minutes to pack. He starts talking about destinations, Vegas maybe, or L.A., sparkplug cities full of attractive people rushing around in androgynous blushing hordes.

"Don't get lost out there," I tell him softly, and he finally looks at me, still smiling. I didn't need to warn him. He doesn't live by any set of rules that I'm familiar with. He's always on the outside of everything. I don't want to say goodbye to him. But there's a little something inside of me that says I'm going back to school, and my heart has clamped around it like an oyster.

"Let's take Penelope swimming," he says.

As it happens, despite the fact that we found Penelope at a lake, she doesn't like the water. The sticks that Brandon has thrown into the lake have gone un-fetched.

"Go get it, girl," he says encouragingly, but she lingers knee-deep in the water and watches the limb bob slowly and float away. Then she barks at it. "So much for bravery," Brandon smiles.

"Maybe she just doesn't see the point," I say.

He strips off his shirt. "Maybe she only learns by example." I watch him take off his shoes and socks, then finally his jeans.

"Great," I say. "Let me go find a stick and I'll throw it for you."

Five minutes later, I've been wrestled out of my clothes and we're both in the water, with Penelope yipping at us from the shore. We swim for a while, calling to her, until we're winded and bracing ourselves against a floating dock.

"I don't think she's coming in," I say, watching her trot nervously from one end of the landing to the other. Brandon isn't listening. He's underwater somewhere, and when he pops up, he asks me what it was like to be the one to tell Terran about Joey.

Before I can answer he says, "It was my idea you know, that you be the one to tell her."

"Why?"

"Because Joey couldn't. Because he might have just gone on the way he was forever. Or worse, he might have just stayed with her." He lets go of the dock and starts to backstroke toward the shore. I follow. Penelope shies away from our dripping bodies like we might use her for a towel. We head over to the Chevy parked under the trees and there are a few shirts in the backseat. I hop up onto the trunk and wring out my hair, watch him dry off.

"Brandon?"

"Yeah?"

"Am I a good person?"

He grins, and comes to stand in front of me. "Yes and no. Now stop thinking about Terran and Joey. I only brought it up because I was curious." He kisses me quick, slides his hand along my leg.

"Wait," I say. "Why yes and no?"

"Doesn't matter," he says against my ear. "The reasons are constantly changing. The answer is always yes and no."

"I don't like explanations that don't solve anything."

"That's just the human in you talking," he says, trying to kiss me again but I stiffen, making him groan. "Violet, maybe there is no good or bad. Maybe the concepts of good and bad are too big, and by trying to define them we've just given ourselves something to fight against. One more thing to fight about that we can't win."

"You mean you don't think that we'll ever be transcendent?"

He pulls back to look into my face. "Think of something that's transcendent." As I try to visualize it I see his point. Picture something transcendent and what you get is nothing that's even remotely human. So he's probably right. Because we're all far too attached to our humanity to ever give it up, not even to evolution. Humanity itself has defied its definition, it has become divine, a source of pride, as seen in everything from manifest destiny to that Will Smith movie about alien invasion.

"You need to stop worrying so much about good and bad," he says, "because concepts like that are generalizations. We're limited by our own heads. We can't grasp the enormity of life, so we have to exist within generalizations."

"We want the truth," he says. "We want reasons, but the moment we find them we'll know that it isn't The Truth, that it isn't The Reason. Because it's all perception. It's all perspective."

"Aren't you just generalizing now?" I ask.

"Yes. That's the point. Truth, The Point, The Reason, they only exist in those words. No other words can contain them." He grins. "Now let's do it."

I laugh and he kisses me. He pulls my hips toward him, his hands cool from evaporation.

"You're not coming with me, are you?" he says softly, and I run my fingers through his drying hair. I don't know how he knows, but he's right. I can't. Because something has shifted, something subtle. I've been waiting for something to happen, maybe something like Brandon, just standing suspended, unable to choose between earth and sky. I've been sending my mind out ahead of me like a falcon from my wrist, hoping that it would come back one day with something other than old dust.

All of my worries really stem from only one uncertainty; the uncertainty of the future, time that we can't get hold of, uncontrollable and frustrating, when we can so easily mold the past to our liking. And my fear is that the future is a myth—that it will never arrive, that it only becomes the present and loses its magic.

But the future is inevitable. Every day it is here and every day it is coming, and it's no longer a push but a warm weight, like time itself brushing past my face. I can walk through it like white sheets on a clothesline, and someday it will bear me down in sedimentary layers. The idea of something that must go on is comforting, and for a moment I am without fear; we are without fear when time isn't chasing us.

The future will come whether I am walking to greet it or sitting on a chair, and I want to believe that this moment, this tiny clear moment I can catch, just this once, but Brandon was right when he said that I couldn't keep them, and I know too much now about the nature of forgetting. I reach my hand out to touch his face and shake my head. He holds me tighter and I realize, maybe for the first time, that all of my daydreams have been of the past.

◆◆◆

My father is reading a novel in the late afternoon light when I come into the den, my clothes squishy and smelling like lake. He glances up once and then back down. I lean against the wall and wonder how long he'll let me stare before he sighs and says,

"What is it, Violet?"

I smile. Twenty seconds. "I'm going back to school, Dad."

He puts down his book, something old and bought primarily because it looks good, maybe David Copperfield or something.

"That's great. What's your major?"

"Paranormal psychology." I grin and he scowls.

"That's not a major, Violet."

"It isn't?" I smile, going over to kiss his frustrated cheek. "It should be. I'm going back tomorrow afternoon. A little early." I hear a shuffle and turn to see that my mother has come into the den, a pretty petite picture in tan slacks and a pink sleeveless blouse.

"Violet," she says, "You aren't serious about that degree."

"If I were it wouldn't matter. Because barring getting hit by a bus, I'm going to change my career at least five times over the course of my life."

They're looking at me like I've lost my mind. Maybe I have, because I pulled that paranormal psychology thing out of nowhere. They tell me it's impossible. That I have no idea how long it takes to carve a place for myself within a profession. I head to the door and open it, ready to walk to Terran's mother's house. I look back at them, and I wish that after I was gone they both wouldn't talk about me like I was the failure of the other one. But this is how parents are. "Guys," I smile. "I know exactly how long it takes."

◆◆◆

When I get to Terran's mother's house, Mary, the housekeeper, ushers me upstairs without calling up to Terran that I'm here, so I give a quick knock at her door.

"Yeah," she says from inside.

When I go in, I think for a minute that she must have read my mind. There are suitcases open and half-filled on top of the bed. Her clothes are spilling out of the closet and most of her drawers are ajar. She comes out of the closet with her arms full of jeans.

"Violet, hey," she says when she sees me, and then goes back to work, folding things into cases. "I'm glad you're here." She stops moving and looks around, blows wispy hairs out of her face. "I—I was going to call you tonight; I was going to stop over." She couldn't have been planning to leave without me. I don't care who I let borrow her car. So I start talking.

"Well now that I'm here I can help you. I thought we'd go back up tomorrow. We could stay with Jenna until the dorms open up, and maybe even after if we don't feel like being communal. We could settle in before the freshman rush. It's not like we'd be missing anything back here." Maybe that's the wrong thing to say, maybe it's an untrue thing to say, but I'm trying to keep my lips moving because she has completely stopped packing. She's just staring down at her hands. "So, I don't know if you want to drive up tomorrow morning, or afternoon, I can be packed whenever—."

"I'm not going back," she says quietly.

I sit down on the bed and start to straighten up a suitcase. She hasn't really been folding things well.

"Did you hear me?" halting my nervous movements.

I look at her. She's in her pajamas at 6:30, and she hasn't got any makeup on. Her hair is up in a twist sticking out every which way. In all the slumber parties we've ever had she's never looked like a mess.

"I did hear you, but it's ridiculous," I scoff. "Of course you're going back. You're in the top ten percent of your class. What, did you transfer somewhere and just not tell me?"

"I'm going to Europe with my grandmother," she says flatly.

There's a sick panicky feeling growing in my stomach it comes from not wanting to go without her. "Why?" I ask. "Is she dying?"

She laughs weakly. "No. I'm pregnant."

I blink. "Get rid of it." I reply, shocked at my response.

I'm not ready for her glare. "How can you say that? 'Get rid of it.' That's so irresponsible, Violet; I'm pregnant, and now I have to deal with it." Then, almost like an afterthought, "It's not like I meant for it to happen."

"Yes you did," I say, surprising even myself agin. "You're not an idiot, some part of you did, and now what are you doing? Going to Europe? Why? You could finish out the semester for sure then take a leave of absence, your mom could hire you a nanny or something if you wanted to keep it that bad—."

"No!" she half shouts. She must have used that same desperate, stubborn tone with Meredith, and what guts that must have taken, to stand before those fangs with all her veins exposed. "You're just scared to go back by yourself, but you'll be fine. You must've picked a major—what is it?" She has changed the subject.

I shake my head at her. "I'm not thinking about that; I'm thinking about you," I say. I'm thinking about her and she knows it, but her eyes are so shameful that I know this was no accident, not really. I wonder when the idea popped into her head—that she might be able to shrink into the recesses of domesticity, that she could tell herself that life had beaten her down, had boxed her in, when it was really she who had given up. When did she start thinking that it was easier than the fight, even though someday she might roll over at 35, swarming with children, with the light gone out of her eyes.

"Maybe it'll call you Aunt Violet," she says to me incredibly, and part of me wants to hit her. Her eyes look so crazy with relief and shock that she wouldn't feel it—she wouldn't hear it if I told her that nothing had changed—she was still the girl with all the choices.

"Why did you do this?" I ask softly.

She shrugs, a disgusting movement of her shoulders. "I love him," she says. I know that she does, or at least she thinks she does, but just the same that phrase irks me now, less a declaration than a justification for all of the stupid things she's gotten herself into. She says it again, to no one in particular, and those lovely little words, once so ideal, are now a destructive little crutch.

I say, "Okay fine, Helen of Troy," but the reproach has no bite; I've made her case for her. Because this is what love has always done. She is blameless.

I ask her how long she's staying away. She shrugs again. I know that it'll be long enough for Joey not to put two and two together, and that's a long time.

"I won't see you," I say she gets frustrated and goes back into her closet. She tells me in a light tone of voice to stop being so dramatic—friendships break apart every day. She says that it's happening to millions of people right now, while we're standing here packing. She says that it's relatively unimportant.

I'm sick of her outreaching brain, her wide angle view of the world that makes things so trivial, like even the life inside her belly is trivial, barely a blink in a place so full of birth. But she has to say that. Because every day she fights the feeling of being small, and that fight has left her with no options. She's pregnant because she had to be, because she needed to bring life close and make it real, and now it is the only thing before her. And if there are regrets, when she's tired of diapers and Cheerios in her hair, she's clever enough to justify them away.

"Listen, Violet," she says, coming out with her arms full of shirts. "I've really got to pack. I have to be to the airport by eight with all of those extra security checkpoints."

"Okay," I say and stand up. I look at her hard, my imagination making her shed her pajamas, making her smooth her hair and brightening her face. But I know that I've lost her. Seven years played down to this moment. I open the door.

"I'll call you," she says and I nod. She will call, for a while. Before we salt the earth between us so that the ground can lose its memory. We'll forget that we once held hands as two sides of a triangle, and that it was once the most important thing to us. And soon, too soon to be fair, new friendships will seem better and more important. That's how it has to be; it's how our brains keep us from going insane over what we've lost, or what we've given up. But the necessity of forgetting is the saddest thing about being human.

She stuffs another shirt into her suitcase and sighs. "I hate airports. They're the saddest places in the world. No one ever goes there to *go* there. No one ever stays."

I don't say anything back. She was talking to no one anyway.

I leave Terran's room. Leave her house. Shut the door. Walk away. It's a quarter mile before I can think of anything beside her face. And when I can, I shake her off like a bird shakes water off of its feathers. That's step one.

◆◆◆

In the kitchen the next morning, my cell phone rings and I jump to answer it, give a few quick yeses and then go up for my two bags. I'll send for the rest of the boxes later. When I get to the door my father stops me, my mother behind him, for once they're a united front.

"You can't go back there without any idea of what to do," he says. I hear Brandon honk from the driveway and open the door.

"I told you yesterday," I response confidently.

"Violet, what is the matter with you? You're 19. I think as I rush for the door. You're running out of time." What a stupid thing to say. There's never an end to time, that's what makes it so hopeless, what makes it so possible. My dad's face is red. He can't stop talking. Won't I ever stop daydreaming and decide on something? He's almost yelling and my father doesn't yell. He's scared for me. And of me. But I'm no longer afraid.

"The only thing that's important about time is not wasting it," I say into his incredulous flushed face, and he says, "Exactly!" Except that we have different ideas about what constitutes waste. He thinks that I'm being ridiculous. That life's too short for all this. But life is only too short when you've found what you seek. Life is too long to bear it in a trap. I suspect that he is unhappy. I want to tell him to break out I'm young, and for that reason, the thought would be seen as condescending.

He doesn't understand me he says and shakes his head. That's the problem between parents and kids—that nonexistent sparkly dream bridge made of understanding.

"I wish that you did," I say with a look of hope on my face. He can't believe that I'm smiling. His voice is strained, he says yes, he wishes he did too. "Then that's enough," I say, two hugs later I'm out the door.

"Hey," Brandon says as I approach the passenger side of the car. I get in and he leans over and kisses me. He backs out of my driveway and I scratch Penelope's fortune cookie ears. He asks me if I want to stop for breakfast.

"Not right now. We've got a bit of a drive yet."

"You're sure you don't want to come with me," he says staring straight ahead. "We could invent happily ever after, you know."

I smile at him, at his dark hair and dark eyes, at the black dress shirt rolled up to the elbows. He's as close to perfect as I've ever gotten, and maybe we are as close to perfect as can be reached, because I am not Violet-In-Love, I am only in love. I don't know how we've managed it but I'm fairly sure that I won't be able to recall the steps for the next time. He says that he loves me. I hope his face will be etched in my memory for the rest of my life.

When we stumbled across each other three months ago over an innocent cup of coffee, I called him a snapshot of a human being. I wasn't wrong. A summer downpour starts and Penelope barks happily at the windshield wipers as the rain bounces up off the road ahead of us and runs down the side windows. When I reach back to pet her, I can see his bags in the backseat, one knapsack and one duffel bag, stuffed full with all of the clothes he is not using now. He will drive me to school, drop me off and wave goodbye. Then he will head west towards the setting sun. I think of Joey, maybe at the gorge, missing us already, or maybe not, maybe he is in Julia's bed. I think of Terran, her brave face looking forward in the clouds, somewhere high above our heads, above the sea. And then I think of me, in this car. Moving fast through the rain with the trees whipping by, their leaves bright green with water. Blurry.

Beautiful.

About the Author

Sleep Walk Society is Kendare Blake's debut novel. She was a Momaya Press 2007 prizewinner, and is published on various sci-fi blogs. Her hobbies include running, ice hockey, tennis, and horseback riding, reading and going on crazy quests to save turtles.

Blake was born in Seoul; South Korea She earned her B.S. in business administration/finance from Ithaca College in New York and a M.A. in writing from Middlesex University in London, England and Cambridge, Minnesota. She now resides in Lynnwood, Washington with her husband.

Sleepwalk Society, Kendare Blake's new novel, is full of brilliant writing. Touching and sad at times, funny at others. A young writer with a talent to watch out for.

—Vivian Hassan Lambert

Violet is no cardboard heroeine. She is concerned more with figuring out herself and her world than with vampiric tonsil hockey—and so her voyage of self-discovery is at its core more painfully, poetically real in its simplicity that any epic romance could ever be. A rawly realistic depiction of teenage life.

—Tara Isabella Burton

Blake writes with graceful subtlety and insight as she creates a complex and intriguing cast of characters, most notably Monroe, who is wonderfully vulnerable and honest as she navigates the difficult journey toward independence and self-discovery.

—Jayne Pupek

Printed in Great Britain
by Amazon

65597561R00104